SPIRIT OF
CHRIST

SPIRIT OF
CHRIST
EXPANDED EDITION

DON DI SPIRITO

ReadersMagnet, LLC

Spirit Of Christ
Copyright © 2021 by Don Di Spirito

Published in the United States of America
ISBN Paperback: 978-1-955603-31-7
ISBN eBook: 978-1-955603-30-0

All rights reserved. No part of this publication may be reproduced, stored in a retrieval system or transmitted in any way by any means, electronic, mechanical, photocopy, recording or otherwise without the prior permission of the author except as provided by USA copyright law.

ReadersMagnet, LLC
10620 Treena Street, Suite 230 | San Diego, California, 92131 USA
1.619. 354. 2643 | www.readersmagnet.com

Book design copyright © 2021 by ReadersMagnet, LLC. All rights reserved.
Cover design by Ericka Obando
Interior design by Renalie Malinao

Dedicated to

*The Blessed Mother through whom
The Christ took on our humanity,
To make it sacred,
And to her faithful spouse Joseph,
The humble and silent worker.*

Special Acknowledgement
Conversations in the Spirit of Christ

Spiritual conversations that I was privileged to have with Fathers Austin Walsh, S.T. and John Mc Spiritt, S.T. of the Missionary Servants of the Most Holy Trinity at the Trinity Missions' headquarters in Arlington, Virginia served as the impetus and substance for much of these writings. I am deeply grateful for the Nativity that the Trinity Mission fathers graciously provided. Their generous hospitality, sharing and spirituality permeate these writings.

Also reflected are the spiritual conversations that I have been privileged to have with others through the years. They include: the Woodstock Theological Center Fathers John Haughey, S.J. and Gerry Campbell, S.J; the Centering prayer group meetings and retreats led by Abbot Mark Delery, O.C.S.O. at Our Lady of Holy Cross Abbey in Berryville, VA, as well as the Northern Virginia Centering-Contemplative Prayer Group hosted by Jerry and Bonnie Makowka; Desert Father Eugene Romano of the Hermits of Bethlehem in the Heart of Jesus in Chester, New Jersey; the Heart of Jesus Charismatic Prayer Group of Northern Virginia; the EPS (Education and Parish Service) program brothers and sisters associated with Trinity University; the Adult Scripture classes at St. Michael Church; colleagues and friends committed to trying "to do what Jesus would do" in helping those in need through the Annandale Christian Community for Action (ACCA); Kim Barker-Brugman who highlights the importance of Christian unity and Barbara Sanders the importance of prayer life; and the home conversations with wife Mary Lee and daughter Lee Ann, my brothers and sisters, extended family and friends, especially Frank Spicer. For this abundance I give thanks and pray that the gifts received are favorably reflected and further shared through these writings as the conversation in the Spirit of Christ continues.

Don Di Spirito
Baptism of Our Lord Feast
2008

Contents

Introduction to Expanded Edition xiii
Prologue xv

Turning to the Spirit Within 1
Becoming One Within 5
Living in the Truth 7
The Continued Creation Within 10
Simplicity of Life Style 14
The Simplicity and Salvation of Each Day 17
Turn to Christ, Word of God 20
Live and Rest in the Reality of Christ 23
Creating a House of Prayer and Love 25
To Pray is to be Changed 27
Prayer: Being Present to God's Isness 29
An Eternal Perspective and Experience 33
The Mystery and Reality of Prayer-Filled
Relationship 36
Life is a Mystery to Live in Christ 39
The Joy of Mystery 41

All is Gift	44
Becoming Rich through Poverty	46
The Many Rooms in God's Mansion	48
In the Seeking is the Finding	51
Following by Letting Go	53
Let God be Victorious in All Things	56
What Kind of Love is This?	59
Be Where We Are	61
A Life Pure and Simple	63
Enlarging the Face of Christ Amongst Us	65
Peace: the Gift, Guide and Measure	67
The Right Connections	71
Jesus is Newness	75
The Humble Crown	77
The Heart and Cross of Jesus	79
Partnering with Christ Jesus	82
Our Master's Voice	85
Walking the Road of Holiness	87
Christ is the Vision, Portrait and Focus	90
The Holy Spirit Must Act	94
The Oil of Gladness	96
The Way Home	99
The Gift and Reality of Love	103
Called to be Loved	106
A Tighter Grip	108
The Talent to Remain in Christ	110
Moving Prayerfully in Heart	115
Must Surrender to Conquer	117
Releasing the Power of Jesus' Teachings and Presence	119

The Spark of Holiness 122
Feeding on the Living Bread 125
A Wide Call and Narrow Path 128
Only a Reflective Life is Worth Living 132

Epilogue 135

Resource and Reference

An Anatomy and Discussion of Prayer

The Power and Many Faces of Prayer 141
Distinguishing Main Lines of Prayer 143
Simple and Infused Contemplative Prayer:
Dimensions and Methods 145
Centering Prayer 147

Annotated Reference List of Related Readings 151

Living in a World of Contingency and Upheaval . . . 159
Living in a New World 163
The Spirit of Christ 166
God's Grace and Love 167
Solidarity of Goodness Grows in our Land 169
A Christ Centered Way Appears 171
Jesus is the Word of God 173
His Words of Eternal Life 175
Finding Heaven in Christ and Discovering Him
in Each Other 178

Introduction to Expanded Edition

Spirit of Christ *is a scriptural and spiritual guide for Christians seeking a deeper and fuller understanding and experience of the Spirit of Christ in daily living. The first edition published in 2008 presented over forty dimensions of faith working through love in a Christ-centered life. It is still a Christ-centered world for those who believe, have hope and love.*

This expanded 2021 edition presents a view and interpretation of the current world and Pandemic that has us living in a so-called new world. The expanded edition addresses how God is calling us to better see and serve the current world and concomitantly the Kingdom and Presence of the Spirit of Christ and Christian protocols, overcoming what surrounds us by what is in us. There are no people exempt from the dangers of the Pandemic. We are called to help one another. As followers of Christ Jesus we place our trust and belief in the Holy One. Praise God!

Since 2021, a number of vaccines arrived changing the course of the virus, providing the protections needed for the public to proceed with confidence in the social order, while responding to the protocols of the scientists like Dr. Anthony Fauci who have light to how we are to walk and believe in face masks and other protection against the COVID-19. They are being acknowledged with honors as more and more are securing the vaccine. We are indebted to them and our Government. All are most thankful for the many dedicated scientists and medical doctors that have produced effective drugs and treatments that have substantially lowered the death rates for millions of citizens across the globe. It is our good fortune that many drug companies and scientists have come to further expand the drugs and protocols available to overcome the deadly disease. The medical and social wisdom articulated through the media avenues with learned, wise voices, the likes of Dr. Fauci and his associates who have steadily subdued the high rates of COVID, reaching now to the 5 year olds. Though living in a new World it continues to be a better and more protected place for all. Dr. Fauci who is Director of the U.S. National Institute of Allergy and Infection and has been for many years, is also Chief Medical Advisor to the President of the United States Joseph Biden.

Prologue

The Spirit of Christ is the love of God poured forth into our hearts (Rm. 5:5). It is the greatest gift that we can receive and give to others. It is also the greatest challenge that each of us will encounter in our lives. Who we are and what we become individually and as a people are linked to this challenge.

To hold Jesus as our only ideal is an awesome responsibility. Yet in reality it is our only real measure of who we are called to be. Our spiritual lives are woven with this response and identity if we choose to accept the gift of Christ and be known as Christians. In this regard, Thomas Merton, the Cistercian monk of literary and spiritual renown, reminds us that there can be no true spirituality apart from the love of Christ Jesus.[1]

Faith working through love (Gal 5:6) in a Christ-centered life is the essence of this book. Our share in the mission and glory of Christ is to make known His holy

---

1 Thomas Merton, Thoughts in Solitude, Farrar, Straus & Cudahy, N.Y. 1961, p.36

presence through the power of His love poured forth into our hearts.

While this writing is spiritual in nature, it is also existential, experiential and personal because we strive to follow and make known the truth and love made incarnate in the person of Christ Jesus. We share this challenge and walk together.

You were within me...
Beauty ever ancient, ever new,
Late I have loved you!

You were within me,
But I was outside,
And it was there
That I searched for you.

You were with me,
But I was not with you.

I have tasted you,
Now I hunger and thirst for more.

You are my physician, I your patient.
And my hope lies only in your great mercy.

——From the Confessions of St. Augustine

Turning to the Spirit Within

Turning to the Spirit within is a radical turn of mind and heart. It was for St. Augustine and it is for us. Remaining in the Spirit of Christ is ever more challenging. Yet it is the most compatible way to our true self and fullness of life. This simple turning to acknowledge and receive God's gift of His interior presence changes our vision, attitude, heart, mind and walk in life. Having made this turn, there is no need to make other turns. Rather we can begin to seek experiences, relationships and activities that are ever more compatible and in harmony with our interior life, focus and grounding. In so doing we nourish our growth and strengthen our gaze. We can be alert for bridge-making experiences and relationships that complement our deeper life experience and affirm our true self rather than allow worldly-minded objectives and standards to shape, rule, confuse and abuse our lives. *Do not conform yourself to this age but be trans-formed by the renewal of your mind (Rom 12:2).* It is the transforming power of the Spirit within, the victorious experience of the Risen Christ that transforms our vision and goals, mind and heart. It is the Christ way, life and truth that we desire, seek and participate in. And it shapes the decis-ions, core and actions of our everyday life. Let us explore this life in the Spirit of Christ together.

In all honesty, we can neither deny, suppress nor negate the life within: the deeper reality of who we are before God. The God of love who created us silently awaits us deeply within. It is for us to embrace His presence in faith and be embraced by His love. This deep love is within us and at the same time transcends us. It is God-given and given for His glory and incarnate growth amongst us.

That which God plants within is meant to grow until it becomes visible in what we do and say. Our challenge is to forge a better unity between the reality and truth of our silent inner life with the activity and language of our daily life. In this unity, we find the reality and joy of kingdom celebration.

This lamp of God's love and light within is not to be hidden under a bushel of possessiveness and fear (cf. Mk 4:21). The gift freely received is to be given freely (cf. Mt 10:8). It is to be given away so that the abundance *within* can realize even greater abundance *amongst* us. The living water within is meant to become part of the ocean of God's presence every-where. The simplicity and peace within are meant to be enlarged by being woven into the fabric of daily life (cf. Is 54:3). The Bread of the Word and Eucharist received is to be further celebrated in our daily lives, filling us and the world in which we walk with the Christ-Presence, the Bread of Life, and completing the celebration that comes to us from the altar of God. St.

Augustine exhorts us to *become* what we receive and to give what we receive to others in the holy name of Jesus.

An interior and reflective life is critical if we are to compare ourselves to the only measure that really matters: Christ Jesus. What activities, desires and behavior nourish a closer walk and comparison to Jesus? What carries us further away from Him? What affirms our relationship with Him? What hinders and diminishes a more intimate and peace-filled walk with Christ?

There is need to look honestly at the reality of our lives: the commitments, responsibilities, desire and use of our time and resources. How are they reflecting gospel values? What can be changed or refined to better reflect Jesus in our daily lives? What small steps can be taken that will move us in a more Christ-like direction and manner of life? These small steps can effect big changes in us as well as those around us, if we are willing to be open to the change within us and the change that can come about through us.

It is the Spirit's mission and power to form Christ within us. With Mary and the saints, it is for us to say *yes* to it. But it is not easy to keep saying *yes* in all things. It is not easy to keep responding to its demands. It never will be. The gift is simplicity. The challenge is to live it again and again, day by day. The talent is to live it gracefully and peacefully.

"Simple souls are not meant to follow complicated ways," St. Therese Lisieux instructs us.[2] Jesus walked a simple path. We are invited to do likewise. It entails a simple but prayerful embrace of our present life. There

---

2   St. Therese Lisieux, *Story of a Soul*

is need to look and work at these present realities in the light of Jesus' teachings, grace and example. Like us He suffered. But now He is risen. Like St. Paul and the saints we too have been and are being crucified with Christ. The realities of our present life provide the means of dying to selfishness, our imagined self, and self-centeredness. But in so doing we can begin to say with St. Paul, "I live no longer, but Christ lives in me." (Gal 2:19-20) We too can become victors in and through the power of the Risen Christ. It is not necessary to prove ourselves to the world and its ways. Rather our goal, means and end are to know, love and live Jesus now and forever. Our wealth is Christ's merciful love and holy grace that comes to live in our poverty.

Having received such generosity of love, we can come to celebrate our Christ-endowed self and begin to recognize in the mirror someone whom Jesus has deemed worthy of creation, redemption and likeness. Realizing such acceptance, we can gladly extend it to others. In this Jesus becomes all in all: We are His *living* body, His corpus. We are not His corpses. Our dignity is rooted in the living, victorious God. Our inner words thoughts and powers begin to take on *one* word, thought and power: *Jesus!* He is enough. He always will be. It is for us to remember who we are and whose we are. We do not own Christ. By grace we simply belong to Him. That is enough!

Lord Jesus it is enough for us to claim you as Victor. In your victory we, who choose you and are chosen by you, are victorious in all things. May we better access the kingdom within to better proclaim it amongst us.

Becoming One Within

In this process of becoming one *with* and *in* God, there is of necessity a letting go of the false controlling self and walk, and an opening to the true self and walk. That is to say, there is a walking away from the false, generating self and a walking toward the true self that can only be found in God and His will for us as found in the realities of our every day life. God is truth and He can only embrace the truth that is found in us.

When we are thinking, talking and walking right, our mind, lips, heart, and feet are in synch. There is rightness, a fit that is right. This rightness is God's affirmation of Himself within us, and our acceptance of the simple reality of who we are and where we are. Without this rightness and presence there is no peace. There is no wholeness. Our life, desires and attention are fragmented. There is no conformity with who and what God calls us to become and be *(with and like Him)*. We are made by God to image Him, and it is for us to let go of all the distortions that we have made in our lives, imagined or otherwise. And so we listen as the Spirit leads and transforms us within, as we respond to the activities, thinking and voices that we see, hear and reflect upon in the course of our daily lives. Which ones really fit us? Which ones only fit the vision that is in another's eyes and mind? Which say "This is really me!", and which a simple and uncomplicated *yes* affirms it? The clarity and fit conform to that which each of us has come to know and experience to be true within.

In the interior life, the knowing and experiencing are one. As such, we are able to discern and realize deeply within which things, people and activities embrace us with whole-ness and rightness. Conversely we can begin to identify which things further complicate, fragment and dilute our lives and the peace that God desires for us.

The gift that we have to claim and give to others is our true self not the false self. As we gain a better sense of the true self and lifestyle, we become more endowed with that to which God calls us. And our voice, vision and life become more vibrant and alive in Christ and before others.

Lord only in you do we find truth and wholeness of being. Help us to honor this in our movements, relationships and choices in life. In Your light may they become right.

Living in the Truth

The base of humility is truth. Our true self is the one who stands before God, naked but not ashamed. It is for us to humbly recognize and celebrate this truth that is ours before God. Our gifts and shortcomings serve to manifest this truth. And in the acknowledgement and employment of this truth, we are brought to new life. It moves us from paralysis to advancement in the Spirit, from darkness to light. In acknowledging and accepting shortcomings, we are able to disarm the conflicts and violence that are rooted in pride. And in employing our strengths and gifts, we are able to advance the common victory to which we are called as a society of Jesus.

Every perfect gift is from above (Jas 1:17). There is no need for us to impress others. God will impress others with the humility and simplicity that are rooted in His gifts and holiness. Our only boast is in the Lord (cf. 1 Cor 1:31). There is no need to defend our pride. Without God we are nothing. How can one defend nothing? There is nothing to defend. Through humility and meekness we are in harmony with the spirit of truth residing in our hearts. We are in harmony with the heart of Jesus, humble and meek (cf. Mt 11:29).

There is no freedom, unity or real life without truth. Therefore it is critical for us to face and know the truth of our lives in all of its giftedness and shortcomings, strengths and weaknesses, struggles and gains.

In living this truth we become free and real rather than manipulated and false. The fundamental choice is to live our lives from within where we find and hold the true self, or live an externally driven life that spins and moves in accordance with the swirling winds that surround us. That which violates the humble truth within is not worth having, regardless of the adulation of the crowds and labels of success they inscribe upon us. The challenge is to remain rooted in the true self, the heart of Jesus, making this the crucial and integral aspect of all situations, circumstances and history in which we find ourselves.

The true self rooted in Christ is the gift, worth and value we have to offer each situation and circumstance. Does this make us the center of the world? Absolutely not! It makes Christ the center of the world, which He is! The reality we know deeply and live truthfully is the reality of Christ within us. It is the crucified but now risen and victorious Christ that we celebrate. He is the One who has irrevocably joined humanity and divinity, living within yet transcending our humanity. It is in Christ Jesus that God took on humanity, and our humanity became linked to God forever. It is no longer a history of humanity alone but rather it is of humanity now living in the year of the Lord,

A.D., *Anno Domini*. Because of Christ, humanity can no longer plead ignorant of God's role and place in the history of mankind, unless one has never heard of Christ for that would be invincible ignorance and thus not accountable.

We can no longer be separated from God. Only sin can shield us from God's grace-filled presence and suspend His goodness and collaboration. Though humanity remains humanity and God remains God, we are invited through grace to participate ever more fully in the divine life. We are sinners but we are redeemed sinners capable of living in, through and with Jesus on earth. Like the prodigal son, our Lord waits for us to turn from sin so that He may embrace us with His cloak of forgiveness and grace, and take us into the banquet of communion. It is in this communion, this embrace, that the loneliness, exile, bitterness, complexity and turbulence of misdirected values and perceptions are swept away and the sea of life becomes calm and right again. We are given a taste of the eternal homecoming. It is good, pure, joyful, simple and embracive. *"Where do you stay?" the disciples asked Jesus. "Come and you will see," he said to them (Jn 1:38-39).*

Lord Jesus you are the light and truth in and through whom we see and become the truth. Keep calling us closer to yourself where we find our true self, and are set free from the enslavement of the false self. Help us to take the time each day to "come and see" You living deeply within us that we may begin to rest our lives in Your abiding peace and wisdom.

The Continued Creation Within

While we begin to experience the homecoming within, we still remain on the pilgrimage as "saints-in-progress." We are capable of stumbling under the weight of our sins and the sins around us. We are also capable of greater holiness. With our consent and cooperation, God can make us holy. He can take the lump of clay we present to Him and mold it into pottery that is worthy of holding His grace. He is the potter and we are the clay (cf. Rom 9:21). He asks only that we stay centered on His wheel to let Him create something new and beautiful. However we can opt to get on another wheel that will yield a more worldly design, acceptance and acclaim. It is tempting. Yet our leader and perfecter is Christ (cf. Heb 12:2), if we choose right. We are called to be the earthen vessels of water that He transforms into the wine of His holy presence. This is what we have to offer uniquely and powerfully to the world around us. But first we must honor the conditions necessary to become His presence in the marketplace. By staying on our Master's wheel, we are molded by prayer, community of believers, liturgy, Scripture, lives of saints in heaven and in-the-making on earth, trials, sacrifices, sacraments, service...all the elements that our religious-oriented lives embrace. We will look different than the worldly designs. Our aim and means are different. The message to be conveyed is different. It is one of hope not despair, peace not turmoil, simplicity not complexity, order not disorder, calm not anxiety, freedom not control, humility not pride, honesty not guile, Christo-centric not ego-centric, and everlasting light rather than the glitter of the market-place. It is a different design. And so are we if we consent to it.

As our Lord's values and love take form within, they begin to shape our lives. Each illumination of Christ is different when viewed through the window of each of His people. It is important that we honor the unique circumstances and personalities that frame the lives of each saint-in-the-making and follower of Christ. The stars are different and numbered by the Lord who calls each of them by name (cf. Ps 147:4). Each of us is a particular and unique construct and illumination of God. *Like clay in the hand of the potter, so are you in my hand, says the Lord (Jer 18:6).* It is for the Lord to mold each of us and for us to remain in His creative hands and be centered on God. Let Him deal with the contradictions that confront us. Let us to be supple to His holy hands and wise enough to know that He is the Creator of all good and holy things. Let Him smooth out the sharp edges. Let the gentle hands of His holy words and spirit shape us into new people who reflect His creative beauty and purpose. Unless it is God who builds, those who build do so in vain (Ps 127:1). Let Him do it with our docile cooperation and submission. Let Him create and build it one spin, one day, at a time. It is for us to just walk humbly and trustingly, one day at a time. That is enough. That is all there really is: one day! May we live it as a new day, the only day, and perhaps the last day.

Lots of darkness around us? So what? Let it be. Let it further feed the recognition and need for the light of Christ to shine within us and through us, for we hold forth the word of life (cf. Phil 2:15-16). In this regard the darkness can become our friend (cf. Ps 88). God is served in all things if our hearts are right and filled with His inner light.

The Master's hands work freely, gently, wisely and creatively until a just and merciful creation is held in His hands for witness to the world. On our part, it takes time, openness, meekness, endurance and trust for our Master to mold us. Finally the fire of His love will purify and solidify this new vessel through which others and we will drink of His holiness. That which is to be poured forth upon the world is calmness, peacefulness, truth, order, simplicity, holiness...all that is Christ and His way. The gift we have received and are to give is one of friendship, love and prayerful communion. By abiding in His presence, we have Christ to offer to a world that needs to be reconciled, recapitulated and restored in Him as our heavenly Father intends (cf. Col 1:20). Our Christmas gift to the world is Christ Himself: His teachings, way of life and holy healing presence. But the marketplace fashions other gifts that glitter through and with other enticements and social conformities. Nevertheless no matter how a Christ-less world is marketed, Christ remains the gift of light given to the world in the love of the Father to restore and make all things new in Him who is holy and eternal. Only in the light of Christ's incarnate and risen life do we see the true meaning, means and goal of life as God intends it to be. Do we want to be transformed in love? Look to Christ. Do we want to have a just society and peace-filled world? Look to Christ. Or do we really prefer the maddening run to disorder, disillusionment and violence? The choice is ours. The consequences are obvious. We can read about them in the daily newspaper and view them on television.

Lord may we allow you to create something beautiful with our lives and cooperation. It is enough for us to keep our eyes on You and be docile to Your sacred touch each day.

Simplicity of Life Style

Simplicity of life style portrays the Master's hand in our creation. Inner calmness, gentleness, patience, kindness, quiet joyfulness, faithfulness and chastity speak of God's presence, the Holy Spirit, to and through us (cf. Gal 5:22-23). Prayer and reflective contemplative living preserve and strengthen His presence. It sings a mystical song of inner freedom that invites others to the dance of abundant life that is found within and celebrated in the simplicity of life. The challenge is not to get caught up into the web of control and manipulation of others as we minister to their needs in life.

The gift of Christ that we have to give is made possible through inner freedom, a freedom that comes from letting go of control to let God be God to others and to us. It is crucial that we maintain this open posture that brings and sustains freedom. But we cannot control it. Nor can we *make* it happen in others or ourselves. We can only *let* it happen to others and us. In doing so, we can allow the power of divine life to flow in and through us, regardless

SPIRIT OF CHRIST

of events that would otherwise enslave us in fear, anxiety or disillusionment (cf. 2 Cor 4:7-8.)

St. Peter tells us to remain calm (cf. 1 Pt 5:7-8). In view of Peter's performance before Pentecost, this counsel is in itself a miracle.

It shows us what God can do when we let God be God. Jesus tells us not to worry about our lives (cf. Mt 6:25) or what to say (cf. Lk 21:14-15). If our lives are rooted in Christ through trust, we will be calm and free of worry of what to wear, eat, or say. Our task and responsibility of God's gift of Himself is to abide in Him so that calm and peace may abide in and through us. A calm, prayerful, free and chaste mind invites and sustains God's presence. *By waiting and calm you shall be saved, in quiet and in trust your strength lies (Is 30:15).* Through a simple life nourished by Eucharist, liturgy of hours, Scripture, community of saints, prayer and service we position ourselves for this to happen. Prayer-filled reflection on the lives of Christ, the Blessed Mother, St Joseph and all their companions through the centuries, illuminate this posture of waiting, calm and trust. Like the wise virgins we have to remain in calm and wait, fueling our lamps with the oil of prayer and other holy means mentioned (cf. Mt 25:1-13).

When Christ the Bridegroom comes in response to our waiting and trusting posture, we will be ready to go ever more deeply into His presence within us and within our lives. Like the wise virgins, we share the waiting struggle with like-minded brothers and sisters. We do not run off to find other fuel and in so doing miss the Bridegroom who calls us to the wedding. Christ gives us the sacramental and other means of access into His presence, and simply asks us to use them wisely. Those who wait also serve. The One upon whom we wait and trust will come. And He in turn will serve us with the grace of His holy presence and providence.

This grace comes in humble and trust-filled waiting; an open and non-manipulative posture that invites God's deepening presence. We do not and indeed cannot control His sovereign holy presence. His presence is a gift to receive. It cannot be commanded or manipulated. We can only celebrate it with open and humble hearts. A simple life facilitates this.

I find that the more simple and prayerful my lifestyle becomes, the more freedom, calm and peace permeate my daily life. It also clears my vision to see all life around me as it really is rather than as others make it out to be. The facade of status symbols and the enslavement that they embody is stripped away. I realize that I am free of them or at least less vulnerable to become entrapped by them. An inner victory and joy are experienced accordingly. The maddening race to "nowhere" is put aside in order to walk calmly in a deeper and everlasting relationship with Christ who is everlasting and has conquered the world of illusion.

Lord Jesus though we may be surrounded by the complexities and velocity of modern technological life, may we keep our inner gaze upon you and grasp the freedom that a simple life of integrity embraces. We do this with Your grace and thus with grateful and joyful hearts.

The Simplicity and Salvation of Each Day

We encounter the Risen Christ in the simplicity of each day. *Behold now is a very acceptable time: behold now is the day of salvation (2 Cor 6:2).* Through the doorway of each new day, a multitude of questions pass: What grace is being given this day? What grace are we ignoring or offending by our attitude, posturing, paradigms, speech or actions? How are we called to grace this moment or situation through our receptivity to and cooperation with Christ? Is it to be a moment of silence? Or is it a time to be assertive in word or deed? A time to be taught? Or a time to teach? A time to humbly receive? Or are we being called to give of our spiritual, material or professional resources? What is the grace being offered to and through us? And how best can we respond and collaborate to illuminate the Spirit-filled moment?

Obviously there is need to listen to the Spirit within us as the Spirit speaks to our hearts through what is going on within and around us. There is need to examine the intent of what we are doing or want to do. The intent may be good but the timing may not. There may be real abiding desires to do something but not just yet. The Spirit speaks this to us if we listen patiently, humbly and openly. Life seldom follows a steady course. Sometimes it tends to become fragmented and scattered. Though these different experiences appear to alter our course, they nevertheless can and do relate to what God is doing or wants to do, if we allow it. God's plans are higher and wider than ours, and embrace a longer spectrum of time. We may grasp only one plan or intent for our lives but God has a thousand alternative plans to get us to where we eventually are to be and become. We may look upon changes, different and thus difficult situations, as interruptions to what we think we should be doing. In reality they can be opportunities to die to our self-perceptions and goals in order to allow a greater perception and goal to be realized by God. With humility and love, God's light can overcome our personal darkness and the darkness of the situation. We can choose to allow God's goodness to embrace each and every situation. We can put aside our way and allow God's way to proceed for the good of all. In freely accepting the crucifixion of doing it our way, God's glory and victory are made manifest. Crucifixion of whatever sort is painful. But it is passing and leads to a higher experience and consciousness that is life giving and victorious. It was true of Christ's crucifixion offered to the love of Our Father, as it is for us in our daily life. It is in the love offering to Our Father that new life comes not only to us but to others as well.

SPIRIT OF CHRIST

The walk of Jesus is our walk (cf. 1 Jn 2:6). His cross and risen victory are ours as well. The gospel is historical but it is being written and lived again in our lives today. The gospel spirit is our heritage to live and proclaim again. In becoming members of the living body of Christ, we have received the opportunity to live His life in our times. We do this by employing His teachings, mission and grace in the time and circumstances in which we are called to live.

So we must look to Jesus. Focus on Him. Receive and imitate His life. Walk with and in Christ, simply and purely this day. And every day!

By putting God's word and presence into practice each day I experience a new vitality and power in my daily life: a generous tip to a house repairman for work well done brought great joy to his eyes and an even greater happiness to my heart; being patient and prayerful in the midst of an insensitive interruption defused an otherwise explosive vocal outburst, creating an environment of forgiveness and calm instead of loud disorder and dismay. The opportunities to turn to the teachings, attitudes, ways and presence of Christ abound in our daily life, shaping our thoughts, actions and reactions. They serve to transport us further on the way of salvation and to prepare the way for others as well. *This is the day the Lord has made. Let us rejoice and be glad in it. (Ps. 118)*

Lord you call us to share in your passion, death and risen life. Help us to see, accept and live all of it, today and always. May we allow the power of your presence to reshape our daily lives into something ever more simple and pleasing in your sight.

Turn to Christ, Word of God

St. Bernard teaches us that we can turn to ourselves to see only despair and disappointment in our many failures and shortcomings. Or we can turn to the Christ living within and find the hope, merciful love and truth we need to see in order to pursue the things that are above.[3] In so doing we become the people we were created to be. So we turn to prayerfully receive the Word, and to walk in His words in order to make incarnate His holy image and presence within and amongst us. When properly trained in the practice and discipline of receiving and living His words, we will be more like our Teacher and Master (cf. Lk 6:40)

It takes faith and the courage of humility to accept and live the words of God, responding to the prompting of the Holy Spirit, our teacher sent by Jesus. There is fear in what these words will do *in* and *to* us as we proclaim them in voice and deed amongst our peers, friends and family. We will sound different and appear different. And

---

3   St. Bernard of Claivaux, Sermon 36.6 on the Song of Songs

perhaps be transported to new and different places. But if we are faithful people, the power of God's love will shine through the darkness of fear as we better embrace and live our Lord's words. It has been said, "Courage is fear that has gone to prayer." So we pray, listen and try to do God's word and *become* His word amongst our peers, friends and family. To become like the Word is to become Christ like and one with Him.

What is in our minds to speak is often judgmental and spontaneously egocentric. But if we move deeper into the heart, there we can find the God of wisdom and eternal words who is loving, forgiving and generous. When our words are united with God and His teaching words, it is no longer "I" who speaks rather it is "We" who speaks. The language is one of acceptance and warmth rather than the cold rationality that gushes forth from the mind alone. In turning to the Christ within our hearts, our words are blessed and transformed by the Spirit and a partnership of love is formed.

In becoming one with God in this way, we receive the power to become one with one another through His grace. Our continuing need is to prayerfully return to the source of the abundant life within us, to the deep well within where we can draw clear, fresh water needed for daily encouragement and refreshment in our lives and the lives of others. Thus Jesus urges us to pray always that we may be mindful of God's presence (cf. Lk 18:1).

We live in very "wordy" world. We are bombarded by spoken, written and video words constantly flashed before us. In this man-made jungle, the sacredness of words has been lost. When our thoughts and words fail to be touched by God within, we all suffer the consequences. St. Paul therefore counsels us to bring all thoughts and things to obedience in Christ (cf. 2 Cor 10:5).

Do our thoughts and words embrace our Lord's teachings and spirit, or do they reflect and multiply the emptiness of the words swirling around us? Are we obedient to the standards of Christ or the standards of a wordy world that fails to be of the Word?

Our affirmative response to these and similar questions are commensurate to the measure in which we faithfully practice His presence in prayer. In and through the transforming power of prayer, we are able to allow God's wisdom and spiritual gifts, His likeness and kindness, to transform a wordy world into an illumination of the Word, Jesus Christ, making it a more sacred place in which to be. In this His glory is known.

Lord Jesus you are the word to be spoken and lived. May our words be rooted in you and give witness to your sacred presence within and amongst us.

Live and Rest in the Reality of Christ

We can count on Christ to give us the best that real life has to offer: Himself. In Him we can rest our cares and hope for He alone is our deep rest (cf.. Ps 62:6). In Him alone do we find Peace and Quality Itself. *To be in Christ means being a completely new creature (2 Cor 5:17).* All else fades in comparison.

We truly walk in His sight. There is no escape from God. God is everywhere, at all times. He is omnipresent and omniscient. If we faithfully acknowledge this, we will walk reverently. Expectantly. Calmly. Humbly. Cooperatively. Triumphantly. Prayerfully. It is a mystery. But we are called to be mystics. We are also called to be prophets who speak and live the word of God. And we are called to live in His holy presence, now and always.

To me life is Christ (Phil 1:21). We live in Him, with Him and through Him. It is to our advantage to acknowledge not ignore this. If we choose to acknowledge this in mind and heart, we will never walk alone. It is for us to walk prayerfully, thus more conscious of His presence. In doing so, a place is made in our hearts and minds that is worthy of His holy presence. Christ has already died for us. Now risen, He wants to live in the Spirit within and through us, making us truly one with Him and each other. But this requires a free and on-going affirmation of His gifted presence, a presence that is acknowledged and affirmed in our thoughts, words, actions and relationships. It is for us to be mindful of Christ always. A recent Doctor of the Church, St. Therese Lisieux the Little Flower, simply instructs us, "Forget all that is not Jesus. And then forget yourself for the love of Him." [4] In her holy simplicity this profound teacher of Christ goes on to say, "Everything brings us to Jesus!"[5] Live in Christ, simply and ever more intensely, ever more prayerfully. All our saints teach us this.

In the Spirit of Christ we find all things: wisdom, under-standing, knowledge, counsel, strength, piety and reverence (cf. Is 11). In Him we are given the way, life and truth of holiness. We should not try to do too much or too little. To be in and with Him is what matters. This is the measure and means of our success. Worldly paradigms of productivity and success fade in comparison. Christ is to be our first love (cf. Rv 2:4). This we must never loose. All else will ultimately be ordered and measured in accordance with His will, not ours; His power, not ours.

Lord Jesus you are the measure and means by which we are to live. All else is of little consequence. In you alone all becomes significant, and all becomes one.

---

4 St. Therese Lisieux, Letters
5 Ibid

Creating a House of Prayer and Love

By receiving and living His words, Jesus assures us that He and the Father will come and make their home in us (cf. Jn 14:23). It is created within us by the Holy Spirit, the mutual love of Jesus and the Father. And it is to be a house of prayer. It is to be place of warmth, filial and intimate love, especially created by the Holy Spirit, who has poured forth the love of God into our hearts (cf. Rom 5:5) There at the center of our being, deeply within our hearts, we are God's friends. There He wants to love us and be loved. He wants to simply *be* with us. There He invites us to rest in His unconditional and mercy-filled love. Christ Jesus wants us to choose and have *the best part:* Himself (cf. Lk 10:42). Having received the warmth of His love, He invites us to serve Him in and through our actions and words that stem from and are sustained by the Source of Love. Without love, the actions and words will amount to nothing lasting (cf. 1 Cor 13). Thus we are asked to pray always (cf. Lk 18:1), which is to say we are to abide in love always, as sons and daughters of the

God of love who makes His home in us. Our attitude and intentions, reflective and spoken words, passive and active postures are meant to be rooted in God who is love (cf. 1 Jn 4:8). Because we are loved, we love. Our love is an extension of and response to His love. The beginning and end and everything in between are to be love, formed and sustained through prayer. Prayer, the communication and transmission of God within us, purifies and frees us to become His presence, His love.

This prayer life takes many forms. It happens in silence and words spoken, community and solitude, passivity and activity, liturgy and private worship, in church and outside of church. It happens by simply turning to God within our hearts and minds to listen to His presence being made known to us in many ways and through many methods. The ways and methods are not as important as the mind and heart that humbly welcomes Him in a spirit of prayer-filled obedience to His holy presence. His presence is a song that is within us and surrounds us in awesome harmony. There should be no discord if we humbly choose to remain in God's presence, prayerfully walking in the Christ life, way and truth.

Lord together may we build a house of prayer and love with the lives you have given us. May our lives resonate your wisdom, compassion and incomparable love.

To Pray is to be Changed

To enter prayer is to invite change. When God dwells in our mind, heart, and activity newness takes place. And newness doesn't happen without something (*someone*) changing. We know that God is Immutable. So it is we, His creatures, who will change. The Messiah comes to free and heal (cf. Is 61:1). New life, energy, perspectives, paradigms, strength, creativity and freshness come as God enters ever more deeply within our minds and hearts and subsequently into our daily life. We are called to say *yes* to His presence and to all that happens as we walk in His presence. Like our Blessed Mother, it is a humble and trusting *yes* to God's will and vision. It is a simple yes to being in His presence with or without understanding all that may be happening in prayer and activity. We simply *let* it happen. We don't *make* it happen. But we let it happen and *go* with it as it happens in a pure and simple trust.

The change happens deeply, slowly and incrementally. Attitude, speech, thinking, behavior, goals and control begin to change through the power of prayer. We find ourselves in less control and more open and free to rest in God's lead in a relaxed, more natural, confident and pristine way. The changes may be so subtle as to be little noticed at first. But change happens as God draws us ever more deeply into His heart as we take on more of His mind and will for us.

Birthing and change imply struggle. The invitation is easier than the response, because the latter involves our decisions, attitudes and actions. It means putting aside many of our proposals in order to be at God's disposal. His ways are not our ways (cf. Is 55:8). But with generosity of heart and mind, we can begin to see or at least accept that His way is the best and most loving way.

Lord, you know all things, particularly what needs to change within us. May we let you change us so that we may better glorify you by becoming one with and in you. In being changed may we so change the world. And may it sing of your goodness and holiness.

Prayer: Being Present to God's Isness

Prayer gives breadth to God's life within. To stop praying is to stop breathing spiritually. It is to die to the life within and succumb to the chaotic, seductive and sometimes violent forces of life lived only externally. "Get a life" should mean to get a prayer life. In doing so, the *better part* is chosen (cf. Lk 10:42). This is not to deny the importance of the active life. Rather it is to choose to live the active life with fuller meaning, value and Christ-centered presence and vision. It is true that God is everywhere. He is *now here*. But if we do not acknowledge and prayerfully experience Him within, he is *no where*—at least to us. Isn't it amazing what happens when we fail to keep the *now* of His presence connected? Suddenly it becomes a *no!* Suddenly there is no sense of God in what we are experiencing. We are no longer *now* connected. But we need to keep the now connected. Prayer connects us to God. So does religion. That is what religion (*Latin: relegare*) literally means: to collect again, tie, bind and connect. We become linked to that which is within us and also that which transcends us. Only God has such qualities. Christ came to *reconnect* what Adam and Eve had broken. And he gave us His church and religion to help us to do this. To exclude Christ from the church and the church from Christ is a mental aberration. The church is the Bride of Christ and there is no divorce. He promised to be with us always to the close of the ages (cf. Mt 27:20).

God simply and purely *Is*. There is no division of time in God. *With the Lord one day is like a thousand years, and a thousand years like one day (2 Pt 3:8)*. God's *Isness* has no beginning or end. *Deus Est:* God Is. In turning from our distractions, we face and enter God's *Isness*. The Almighty is always "there". But God is *now here* when we turn to Him. In prayerfully turning toward God we have, so to speak, made God a part of our time and us. In doing so God's *Isness* has been made our *Isness*, so to speak. But in truth, we are only a part of God who always Is. And we can never escape God in actuality. Only in our failure to acknowledge God does He "escape" our consciousness, attention and reality. Nevertheless God still is and we are always a part of Him in life and death, unless we ultimately choose to live apart from God forever at the end of time. Apart from this unforgivable sin – this rejection and failure to receive God and His merciful love and forgiveness – God's *Isness* is always available to us. The choice is ours to acknowledge or ignore God; to walk with or apart from Him; to say God is *no where*; or to rearrange the "letters" in our life and thinking so as to acknowledge God as *now here* and everywhere. In doing so, we speak and live right.

A pure and facile way to acknowledge and enter God's *Isness* is through the gateway of solitude and silence. Like God, silence simply is. And when we enter this silence alone, there are no audible distractions to carry us away. We simply and prayerfully come to God in what is: Silence.

In this silence our mental pictures and words about God disappear as we let go. We are simply left with God's *Isness* from and through which we derive our true *isness*. There is no need of words or thoughts to transport us there. But there are methods of contemplative prayer (e.g., Centering prayer) to position us to enter the gateway of God's *Isness* through silence and remain with and in Him. In the poverty of our silence and solitude, we receive the richness of God's *Isness*. In the letting go of our own resources, we become absorbed into God's magnificence. In this simple communion we become real, true and whole. There are no differentials as to where God begins and we end. We are now in oneness with Him. Silently and purely we receive and share God's *Isness*.

There is no further need to acknowledge God's presence with words or to construct and define His presence with thoughts. The silence simply opens within us a pure place for God's presence. No need to do anything. Just be in His holy presence. In the stillness of silence, the movement of God's presence becomes apparent and real. We become absorbed in this silent movement, this inner dynamic of Holy Presence that transcends us but also embraces us and ultimately consumes us. The gift received is what we communicate to others in His name and being as part of the divine movement and dynamic. This gift is for us to accept or reject, acknowledge or ignore, celebrate or desecrate.

Through it all, regardless of our choices, God Is. He cannot be destroyed. The only thing that we can ultimately destroy is our souls, if we choose not to be part of this divine movement. It is not something that we earn or deserve. Rather it is a gift to receive and keep in faith with great thanksgiving and care.

Lord in prayer and especially in silence we choose to enter into your Presence. In your embrace love, freedom and newness resonate throughout our inner being and we experience your Isness. Praise you! Thank you!

An Eternal Perspective and Experience

Our life is not just temporal. It is eternal in nature through baptism. As God calls and prepares us on the earthly journey, he also calls and prepares us for eternal life. He is preparing a place for us (cf. Jn 14:2). And that place is with Him, now and forever. The glorified Christ whom we now experience in the Spirit *is* the kingdom. He is the starting point, means and goal of our true life. We find this kingdom within us as we journey in time, and come to experience him fully when we leave time and enter eternity. God's call is to holiness and God's call is irrevocable (cf. Rom 11:29). All of us are predestined to holiness. The question remains before us: Do we accept the call? Do we accept the Christ who lives within us and calls us to His holiness? Do we consent to His presence and movement within us? Or do we race around without acknowledging His power-filled and calming presence within?

God sees things from an eternal perspective. Though experienced in the temporal and perhaps turmoil, His plans for us transcend the present. His plans for us are peace and our welfare (cf. Jer 29:11). To move us in the right direction, He inspires us to do "this" or "that" and, in so doing, grace comes more fully into our lives. One day the "this and that" will disappear and we will be fully consumed in God Himself who simply Is.

This movement does not come all at once. Nor does the Lord's gentle whisper within. When we become still, we begin to hear and sense the movement within us and all around us. Simply, calmly and steadily we move in and with it. And in so doing, the temporal scene begins to change as we change within. It is a less threatening and more welcoming environment in which we move. The judgmental God in mind begins to become the loving and accepting God in our hearts. We belong to this loving God. Our identity and being, hope and trust are in Him. With time, our minds and hearts are moved to accept and live in the presence of this Love who is God. We see differently. Thus we live differently. The rejection is replaced by acceptance, insecur-ity with security, and anxiety with peace. He becomes the cornerstone of our experience. We belong to Him. We are vital parts, living stones, in His glory that has no end. Simply and purely He is our God. We are His people. We *belong* together. We *are* together. And let no man put asunder what was meant for us from the beginning and has been restored to us in Christ, the new Adam. Without this attachment, this secure love, we are left to become nothing (cf. 1 Cor 13). Without this, love and knowledge take on a different meaning and soon dissipate with time. Without this power of God's love within us, acknowledged and accessed through faith, we are left only with our passing humanity. But with this Love power, we are participants in the divine life that has no end. And we gain an eternal perspective and experience.

Lord Jesus may we better consent and respond to your call to holiness and holy presence within so that we may see with your eternal vision and live with you always.

The Mystery and Reality of Prayer-Filled Relationship

Jesus incarnate was a man of prayer and now risen is our heavenly intercessor (cf. Rom. 8:34). We are invited to enter this life of prayer and to breathe the loving relationship of the Blessed Trinity through Christ our High Priest. The receiving is for giving to others. But the giving draws us back to the receiving. In this we become the loving community with the communion of saints in the Trinitarian love community of Father, Son and Holy Spirit. Its essence is life giving. God does not want us to head toward a dead end.

Christ came to give us life, and life abundantly (cf. John 10:10). Therefore, we must ask, "Who and what is putting a spin on our life?" Does it lead toward an end that is deadened by more confusion, emptiness, contradiction and darkness? Or are we experiencing greater inner freedom and genuine joy that display the marks of the Holy Spirit as we engage these activities, relationships and direction?

It is a struggle involving both inner and external dimensions that accompany these questions. But it does lead to life and authenticity. The simplicity needed to get there however is not so simple to apply. Because of the multiplicity, diversity and complexity of life's circumstances, the purity of vision needed is not so clear or easy to attain. It involves personal struggle and purgation. But God heals and gives life-giving grace to make us free to enter the abundant life that the Incarnate Christ came to give us.

God, who is holiness and purity, invites us to Himself. We are asked to respond with a humble and willing *yes* to our loving God. It is an unforced, simple consent that frees us. It also fully accepts the reality of the circumstances in which we find ourselves, as well as our trust in God's power to transform all to the good (cf. Rom.8:28). Through God's embrace and transforming power, we enter a life giving, changing relationship and experience regardless of the circumstances that may very well not change.

Transformation takes place. But it is within us. It is an *inside job* that takes place. The power of the transformation enables us to see and live differently in the particular circumstances given to us. We enter God's peace and God's presence. Together we become one and are in harmony with one another because we are one in harmony with God. The peace and presence are one. We have this peace but in a non-possessive manner. We know and love it without fully understanding it. We keep it by giving it away. We "control" it by not controlling it. It is a paradox. Who can explain such a thing? Who wants to? It is better to experience and *have* it with simplicity, thankfulness and praise than to explain it in a purely rational manner. It is mystery. It touches but transcends our rationality. Yet it is also very real.

Lord Jesus in you we are transformed and given access to the abundance and reality of your kingdom and reign. May we better experience and give witness to this with our lives rather than seek to better explain this with words.

Life is a Mystery to Live in Christ

Life is a mystery to live not a puzzle to explain. Much that happens cannot be fully explained. But it can be fully experienced, if accepted. We are invited to accept and live the mystery of Christ Jesus, once crucified but now risen and victorious. In this acceptance, we experience the divine within us and in our lives. It is the *experience* that matters not the explanation.

Whenever and wherever the divine and the human mix there is mystery. There has to be mystery or there would be no transcendence that reaches beyond our control and limited rational understanding. Otherwise we would be left to our human understanding and limitations. In living the mystery of the Risen Christ, we are raised beyond the mere human experience to a participation in the divine wisdom and life. In this participation in the divine we begin to experience what human perfection, the fullness of humanity, is all about. At the end of our journey in time, the last day, we will see God and be like Him, transfigured into His likeness and brightness. Then we will have no questions to offer or need for explanations. His merciful love will envelop and transform us without end.

It is important therefore to begin to accept and celebrate this infinite merciful love *now*. In accepting this love we are being transformed and can celebrate it by becoming merciful love to others. On that last day, God will thus recognize His merciful love within us and envelop us in it forever. We do not have to explain all of this.

We just have to accept and live it in faith. The acceptance will become the reality in which the love will become the knowledge. The knowledge will become the loving. It is mystery. But the mystery is and ever more will be real. In the loving we will know and be known.

Lord Jesus in loving you we come to know you. In knowing you we come to love you. And in coming to know and love you, we come to know and love our true self.

The Joy of Mystery

There is a joy in mystery that frees us from the obsessive need to have all the answers and understanding, or that we must find and work out the solutions by ourselves. And the key to that joy is found in acceptance in the light of God's abiding presence. In accepting, believing and trusting in God's presence, providence, goodness and love we are no longer enslaved to the necessity of having all the answers and understanding for the circumstances and situations in which we find ourselves. Instead of the pride and control that knowledge seemingly holds, we can choose to humbly accept the situation, let go of the illusion of control, and allow God to do His thing within and amongst us. In this process of letting go and placing our trust in God's providence, freedom and wisdom become operative. We become free to be embraced by the Living God whose will and wisdom are being worked out in us, around us, and beyond us through what is taking place. We often place too much trust in our own immediate understanding, and set about trying to fix things when

God simply asks us to let go and abide in Him rather than our own understanding and facile ability to fix things. Scripture teaches us to trust in the Lord with all our heart and not rely on our own insight (cf. Prv. 3:5). Rather than trying to fix it with our own answers and understanding, our time and efforts can be better employed pondering what God is trying to do and say in these circumstances. And with humble heart and mind wait for God to reveal what He wants for us. But it begins with acceptance and its companion trust. In the humble waiting, the joy of mystery enters.

God's wisdom may show us that the real change required is *in us* and not around us. And then we must allow Him the time and means to change us through our co-operation with His will. Or it may be that the situation itself needs to change but the change is really beyond us. Again there is the need to allow God the time and means to solve the situation in our best interests. It is for us to abide in God, do our best with the available resources, personal and otherwise, and leave the rest to God. God helps those who seek and need His help. Otherwise He lets us do our own thing without His help. The closed door of pride shuts God out as we busily go about solving the matter by ourselves. To allow the change to happen, it is necessary to work *through* our pride and come to poverty of spirit — a poverty that doesn't have all the answers or means needed for change. The Lord honors this self-honesty and dependence upon Him, telling us that blessed are they who know that they are poor in spirit for they will experience the saving power of the kingdom (cf. Mt. 5:3). That is to say, we can have joyous hope in the midst of the mystery of suffering, complexity, and trials if we are humble enough to abide and trust in God. In working through our pride we turn to Him and He fills the situation with His healing presence. However, we must keep in mind our pride still lingers on the sidelines waiting for the next game and trial to begin, so we must always remember to do our best and be humble enough to ask God to help us.

Help us Lord to know that you are with us in all things if we allow humility to open the door to your healing grace. May trust be our strength, and patience our shield as we meet and conquer all things with and through you.

All is Gift

All is gift: But only if we accept it. When not accepted it becomes uninvited burden or an interruption in fulfilling our will. In acceptance it becomes an uninvited opportunity to surrender to God's will. The humble surrender invites God's mercy to shine on our weakness if it brings suffering, and His glory to shine if it brings elation. In either case, when accepted, it spells victory.

Life itself is gift. And all that life brings is an extension of this gift. But to become gift, we must accept the gift regardless of how it may be wrapped in the circumstances through which it is delivered. We will recognize the gift because it comes as the *Present*. The choice is to accept, ignore or reject it as it comes in the present moment. If we realize that it happens in the full sight and knowledge of God, which is true of all things, we should also realize that the gift also brings His merciful loving presence to fill us. With such acceptance, knowledge and vision the gift will carry a ribbon of victory and be magnificently wrapped with God's loving peace.

There may be pain or suffering involved with the accepted present. We do not have to look to God to explain it. He may not even remove it. But in humbly accepting the present, God will fill it with His presence.

The peace of Jesus is won in the present and we will triumph over all these things through Him who has loved us and walks with us (cf. Rom. 8:37). If the present moment is wrapped in pain and suffering, we look to the cross of Jesus and its power to overcome all, even death. If it brings glory we also look upon the cross of Jesus through which it was made possible for us. St. Thomas Aquinas teaches us that "the passion of Christ completely suffices to fashion our lives; for the cross exemplifies every virtue: love, patience, obedience..."[6] In and through all things we follow the crucified but risen Christ Jesus. And we do it with praise and thanks for the power and victory that is ours through Him.

Lord Jesus all becomes gift and victory in you through your cross and risen life. Help us to remember and access the power and victory that only you can ensure.

---

6   St. Thomas Aquinas, Collatio 6 Super Credo in Deum

Becoming Rich through Poverty

When we accept God's sovereign will rather than exercising our own controlled will, we open the door of humility. This humility takes us to a deeper life where trust and faith take over, and knowledge of where it all leads escapes us. This poverty of knowledge and control in turn opens us to receive the purity of God's riches and ways. In our emptiness God's fullness is invited and experienced in our transparency. We acknowledge and accept our poverty in a spirit of expec-tancy and thanksgiving because it invites and celebrates God's presence and promises. *Blessed are the poor in spirit, for theirs is the kingdom of heaven (Mt. 5:3)*. We become poor: But only to become rich. Without acknowledging our poverty, how could we really acknowledge God's richness and our utter dependence?

This poverty of spirit is not something of which to be ashamed or shunned. It is blessed. In the Sermon on the Mount Jesus said that He would bless this attitude. And He does bless it with Himself. Indeed the beatitudes are a portrait of the inner life, the heart, of Jesus. In accepting and living them, we become a portrait of the inner Christ. And we become happy inside because of it. Only a truly humble and poor person can write a sign within himself that says, "I am poor. Please help!" With the courage of faith and blessing of humility, this admission can be held up before God and man. There is no shame. Just reality. Just truth.

With such a spirit and truth, we can truly worship God in spirit and truth as we are called to do (cf. Jn 4:24). And thus we become one with the Giver who transcends our control and understanding, yet humbles Himself to become one with and in us. The humility of Christ was deeply embedded in the spirituality and attitude of St. Francis of Assisi, enabling St. Francis to embrace poverty with his entire life. St. Francis Assisi, Blessed Mother Theresa of Calcutta and many others came to embrace and be embraced by the poverty of Christ that brings with it a richness that the world cannot give. It is a road that the Master traveled. It leads to freedom, fullness and victory.

Divine Master in walking with you through the inner door of humility and poverty we are made rich within. Help us to better embrace the paradox of becoming poor in order to become truly rich, and of becoming empty in order to be fulfilled. May we allow love to overcome all fear in doing so.

The Many Rooms in God's Mansion

Our walk in our own poverty within leads always to God's riches. It is Jesus who prepares a place for us and in this place, this mansion of God, there are many rooms (cf. Jn 14:2). Its construct begins on earth within us. God invites us to be in a room of solitude and silence. There we can be physically still but very active responding to the Spirit's dynamic presence within us. We can enjoy just being alone with God in the unity and peace of the Holy Spirit. In another room of our life's mansion many people are gathered and busily engaged with one another. We can enjoy the dynamism of interacting with them. At the same time, we can also acknowledge the solitude of God's presence within us as we move about the many others. We see the many faces of God reflected in their many faces.

God invites us to a Great Room, majestic and solemn, where many gather but they do so to focus on God and give worship as His church on earth. Here God's gifts of grace, the sacraments, are shared and the glory celebrated.

In Jesus, God becomes the food, light and conversation. He invites us to His Banquet. In communion we receive and celebrate Him. And we share Jesus and His words with one another. An abbreviated and different form of this gathering is celebrated in our families and private homes as well. We also find in God's Mansion work, study, social and as many rooms as there are aspects of our lives. We act differently in each of these rooms yet we are the same person who encounters and experiences them. It is for us to trust in the Mansion of Many Rooms uniquely being constructed for us through our life experiences, and ultimately awaiting us in heaven where *eye has not seen nor ear has heard what God is preparing for those who love Him (1 Cor 2:9)*. It is for us to accept, honor and celebrate the Mansion of Many Rooms in and to which we are invited to live with God. Each of the many rooms is different. But it is the same God and the One Mansion. There are many gifts but only One Giver. Jesus invites us to His banquet, to feed on His Eucharistic presence and holy word – "the edible bread and audible bread," as N. T. Wright calls them.[7] He walks and talks to us in each room of Our Father's mansion. So many different rooms! Yet they are all connected and complementary to one another. Our true self is not found or exercised in just one room. It is the totality of the Mansion of Many Rooms in which our life is found and celebrated. And this mansion is always *under construction*. More rooms are added as life's interest, creativity and communion with God grows. In

---

7   N.T. Wright, Following Jesus, William Eerdsmans Publishing Co. Grand Rapids MI, 1994, p. xi

this construction we also recognize our passage as a person, somewhat the same yet different. We recognize the old and the new. God has and is gifting this passage with Himself. It is for us to walk with grateful, open and loving hearts of praise for the past, the present being given to us, and the Glorious Mansion that awaits us. God is found and celebrated in all of it. And so are we for we are God's children, heirs of Christ (cf. Rom.8:17).

So much is given, Lord, as we move through life's experiences and places with you. And so much remains to be given as you welcome us into the fullness of our Eternal Mansion.

In the Seeking is the Finding

In seeking, St. Augustine tells us, we are already found by God to whom we have turned. "He is found when He is sought," Thomas Merton reminds us, "and when He is no longer sought He escapes us."[8] Our God is a jealous God who wants our hearts, our deepest and true self, not just our occasional attention, fickle commitment or superficial love. *When you seek me you shall find me, when you seek me with all your heart (Jer 29:13).* Jesus assures us that "everyone who asks will receive, and he who seeks finds" (Matt 7:8).

In striving to be God's loving and serving friends, we are the friends upon whom God bestows His holiness. But this holiness is often hidden from us lest we become proud, self-satisfied and end or slacken our striving and seeking. And so the call in Scripture is to endurance, patience and confidence (cf. Heb 10:35-36). But the confidence is not in our ability to grow in holiness. Rather it is confidence in

---

8 Thomas Merton, Thoughts in Solitude, Farrar, Straus & Cudahy, New York, 1961, p. 88

God to bestow His holiness upon us, and our willingness to receive and live His holiness in us. We need not waste time taking measures of our progress along the way. We would only get falsely depressed or impressed. Neither status is pleasing to God. What is of paramount interest and value is our willingness to keep striving to live the holiness that Christ has bestowed upon us. We live this holiness by His call, merits and gift, not ours. *As he who called you is holy, be holy yourselves in every aspect of your conduct (1 Pt 1:15).* So we strive to better accept and live the gift of Christ's saving holiness and to better mirror Him in all things. It is not for us to know how far we have progressed. Lest we become "proud as hell!"

Rather it is for us to humbly acknowledge the gift received that is in progress in our lives. The story is told about one of Thomas Merton's novice monks who said God told him to ask the novice master where he now stood in his spiritual walk. Merton prudently said to the novice, "That is really interesting. Because I was just told that it is none of your business where God happens to have you on your spiritual walk!" Our business is to just keep seeking and believing.

Lord you said to follow not measure. May we better acknowledge and live your holy presence with humility and deep gratitude. And may others come to know that you are a merciful saving Lord to whom we have given our hearts and who lives in our hearts.

Following by Letting Go

We learn to follow His way by letting go. We simply let go of our control, manipulation and plans for our lives. We learn to be still and wait for God so that God's activity within and around us can take place (cf. Ps 37:7). And in loving faith, we accept what God allows and sends our way: The nice and the ice, the neat and the heat, the pain and the gain... all of it! If necessary, we let God tear down in order to build anew. We let God's presence and will be revealed in what *does* happen rather than in what *should* happen. We simply follow by *letting* it happen. We commit our way to the Lord and trust that He will act (cf. Ps 37:5). We already know before hand what He requires of us: *Be just, love tenderly, and walk humbly with God (Hos 6:8)*. We let His words dwell richly in all that we do, say and think (cf. Col 3:16). In doing so we are able to do the just thing in a loving manner, and humbly accept whatever He sends to us each day.

In learning how to follow we can in turn lead others in God's way. The best followers become the best leaders in the divine scheme. It's a humble, attentive and obedient trail with no room for the proud or the slothful. None of it is really easy, though it gets easier as we walk more closely and humbly with God.

We rest in the confidence that God will act and will direct things the best way possible, no matter what we perceive to be "successful" or "best". *Trust in the Lord with all your heart, on your own intelligence rely not; in all your ways be mindful of him and he will make straight your paths (Prv. 3:5-6).* Our trust in God and commitment to live His teachings will give witness to God's love and righteousness regardless of the situations and outcomes. If we are humble enough not to try to control the outcomes and events that enfold before us, God will have the space and time to exercise His control and influence. The reality is that the entire world is really in His mighty hand. Christ has already come and triumphed over the darkness of sin and death. We need to be humble enough to believe and live His victory gained through the cross. We will and do share in His suffering as His body on earth but the end is victory not defeat. Defeat would be to live by worldly standards that bring enticing but fading rewards. It would be to conform to the culture around us rather than be transformed by the power of Christ's saving cross, words, personal example and risen presence. If we walk in His teachings as His living body on earth, God's will is done in our lives and the life of the world. We can't be building walls to keep the world out. There is no *need* to do so. There is no *way* to do so. God will not and cannot be excluded even when others give Him no space or credence.

All is open before God, in His full view. And God will have the final say in all of history.

Lord you know and can do all things. May we be ever more open, submissive and responsive to you in all things. May the peace and order for which the world yearns begin with us.

Let God be Victorious in All Things

It is imperative and in our best interest to acknowledge Him in all things, follow humbly in His way, and let God be God in all things. Because Christ is all in all (cf. Col 3:11). And He is truly with us until the end of time (cf. Mt 28:20). Let the reality of this embrace us, shape our attitude and behavior, and claim the victory already gained. Only in Christ, with Christ and through Christ can this be. St. Peter reminds us that there is no other Name through which we can gain or claim this salvation (cf. Acts 4:12).

It is for us to help bring down the walls and obstacles to the way, life and truth of Christ within ourselves and the world around us. But we tear down only to build up God's kingdom, the kingdom that has come to us in and through the person of Christ Jesus. We should produce enough evidence in our lives that we are God's people and His kingdom is in process within and amongst us. Commitments to honesty, purity and all other aspects of excellence will help to make this happen. Whatever is true, honorable, just, pure, lovely, and gracious gives evidence of God and the kingdom that Christ has brought to us (cf. 1 Phil 4:8).

Man's mind and resources alone will not build a better world or society. Surely the daily newspapers give ample evidence of this. But when joined to God's heart, the heart of Jesus, it will have true life and will prove to be honorable, just, pure, lovely and gracious. We will begin to reflect the kingdom vision and reality proclaimed and lived in Jesus.

There will be victory because there *is* victory. Working from Christ's victory, we move the world toward victory. The obstacles are our sins and mistaken attitudes and perceptions about what life is really all about. In the Sermon on the Mount, Jesus teaches us the attitudes needed in order to be true, just, honorable, pure, lovely and gracious (cf. Mt. 5). The attitudes of Christ, *the beatitudes,* produce the fruits of the Holy Spirit and kingdom life: *love, joy, peace, patience, gentleness, generosity, kindness, faithfulness, and chastity (Gal 5:22).* But these attitudes needed to truly be right are in sharp contrast to the criteria for rising success in the marketplace. Meekness, poverty of spirit, compassionate sorrow, purity of heart, willingness to suffer persecution, and peace making are not the currency that trades well in the marketplace. Like the good coach, Jesus calls us aside to instruct, admonish and refresh us. Then He sends us back into the arena of life to give witness to His counsel and the power of His presence within us. Let us not deceive ourselves, all belongs to Christ: The world, life, death, present or future (cf. 1 Cor. 4:18-23). We are not our own masters regardless of the illusions held before us by a world eager for personal exaltation, gain, and success. We belong to the Lord. The victory is His and it is ours to claim in His Name. It is ours to celebrate in faith and thanksgiving.

Lord you can only be victorious in our lives if we allow it. Help us through love to overcome all fear in developing the attitudes that enable and empower us to be like you. Become our victory now and always that we may boast only of you.

What Kind of Love is This?

What kind of love is this love of God? Look at Jesus and His followers, Saints Francis of Assisi and Anthony and the multitude of holy people who embraced and imaged this love of and for Our Heavenly Father in the Holy Spirit. It includes the way of the cross and its suffering. But it also embraces the joyful freedom of the love within that enables us to choose the way of the cross and follow in the way of the Master. These steps and way of Jesus lead to victory and eternal freedom. They constitute our glory and risen triumph in the *nowness* that begins here and continues forever. *Rejoice to the extent that you share in the sufferings of Christ so that when his glory is revealed you may also rejoice exultantly (1 Pt 4:13).* We follow in transforming steps that make us into the image of Jesus whom the Father already sees within us. One day, we will see Him face to face and fully realize that we are like Him (cf. 1 Jn 3:2). Now we see dimly as in a mirror. Later we will see Him clearly and ourselves in Him. *Then I shall know fully as I am fully known (1 Cor 13:12).*

We cannot make ourselves like Him. Only God can make us like Himself. It is up to God to do it. He has the power. But we have the choice. Do we want (desire) to become like Him: Holy, pure, merciful and loving? With the Blessed Mother as our model and partner, we can say *yes* to the invitation that the Christ be formed within us.

And the process begins. In saying *yes* to His teachings, the Holy Spirit gives life to His words and they begin to dwell richly within all that we do, say and think (cf. Col 3:16). We start to take on the image of the One whose words shape our thoughts, words and actions. Others gain a glimpse of Christ living in and through us as we likewise recognize Christ's traits and goodness in others. In doing so the Kingdom is better realized within and amongst us.

We can also come to recognize Christ through negative lenses as well. That is, we clearly see who and what He *is not* when looking upon violent behavior, distorted values, disordered lives and cultures. In such darkness, the shinning stars of positive traits and values are illuminated. The negative serves as a clear contrast to the positive, making them ever more attractive and bright. Thus we see that in all things God is ultimately served. *We know that all things work for the good for those who love God, who are called according to his purpose (Rom. 8:28).*

Lord your love penetrates all things. Help us to receive, facilitate and magnify your love. May your light shine within and amongst us until we see only your radiance enveloping and consuming us. To your glory let the praise arise, now and forever.

Be Where We Are

To simply be where we are is not so simple. It may be a painful place. The temptation is to flee quickly and completely. Or it may be extremely pleasurable and the temptation is to stay there always. While experience teaches us that pleasure and pain pass on, we have to relearn the lesson again and again. Balance is needed. It is important for us to remember that the affliction will pass as will the pleasure. God is with us whatever the circumstances. Because we are yoked to Him it is a good place to be. The pain will teach us as eloquently as the pleasure. As we are ministered to through His Holy Church we are also called to be Church wherever we are. Remain "churched." Flow with the mind and heart of the teaching Church in the midst of life. Co-create with God an environment of holiness, peace and gentleness, making it a kingdom place and time. *For we are God's co-workers (1 Cor. 4:9)*

It is for us to choose life in the Spirit of Christ and not the spirit of the world, for the Spirit of God within us is greater and more powerful (cf. 1 Jn 4:4). Jesus has already conquered the world through His holy cross and invites us to abide in Him and His victory. In accepting and practicing the wisdom of God we become the wisdom and way. It will bring forth contradiction in the course of life's daily decisions, behavior and thinking. Nevertheless cling to Jesus who is the wisdom of God (cf. 1 Cor 1:24).

Work with Jesus. Proclaim His truth and way that we have come to know, experience and celebrate through Holy Scripture, Eucharist, and His teaching and serving Church. It is for us to grow in and through this until we truly have a living faith and trust in His abiding presence, acceptance and guidance.

St. Peter tells us that though it may be necessary to be sad for a while because of the many kinds of trials suffered, their purpose is to prove that our faith is genuine and will endure (cf. 1 Pt. 1:6-7). So it is for us to be where we are. Stay yoked to the grace of Christ. Remain in His peace and presence within. Remain with the community of saints, the Church militant and triumphant, who abide with and in the Lord. We should not wish to be somewhere else. Just be where we are. Jesus is there too. He will fill the circumstances with His merciful presence and in doing so will transform them. It is for us to remain faithful to Him. He will be faithful to us always.

Lord Jesus, your abiding presence is enough. May we not let the lie of your absence rob us of the faith and reassuring truth of your abiding presence within us right where we are. Help us to better realize that each moment is sacred when we claim your presence in faith. Let us be content to live the sacredness of each moment accordingly.

A Life Pure and Simple

A life pure and simple: It was lived for us by Jesus. Then by the saints who followed: Andrew, Benedict, Claire, Dominic, Eugene, Francis de Sales, Gregory... through the alphabet and centuries they walked the way of the Master. And now our beautified friends and Master call us to live a holy life with them, without end. But it must begin now, in this time. They shine their holy light of constant prayer and inter-cession upon us. Let us be people of constant prayer as well in what we think, say and do. Always with God at the center of our thoughts, intentions and actions, we think, speak and do. Prayerfully, we listen to what God is saying to us and to others. What is the Spirit saying to us? In a word, *Jesus!* "Live Jesus", St. Francis de Sales succinctly tells us. Be prayerful, humble, chaste, selfless, patient, poor, joyful, gentle, pure, meek, obedient, serving, kind, and focused on Father God. Be in the world but not of the world. Listen to Our Father calling us to His holiness through His Son. Let the Spirit of the Son's love draw us more deeply into Trinitarian life.

Having drawn us to Himself and holiness, He can bestow us upon others in His name. Together we join the divine dance of holy love.

Jesus is the same yesterday, today and forever (Heb 13:8). We gaze upon the same Jesus as the saints of old. Like theirs, our mission is to live Him in the fabric of our time, weaving a portrait of Christ that has the same qualities, characteristics, attitudes and holy radiance possessed and expressed by Jesus. We ought to live just as he lived, St. John tells us (cf. 1 Jn 2:6). In doing so, we will rediscover in our times the power of prayer, the cross, Scripture, anointing and sacraments that Jesus embodied and which were embraced by the saints. "Jesus is the life to live. He is the word to be spoken," as a saint in our times, Blessed Mother Theresa of Calcutta, instructs us.[9] The teachings and life of Jesus are what we hold up before the world to see. It is His life that we are to celebrate and replicate. It is His gifts that we receive and share, His call to holiness that we answer, His clarity of vision that we seek, and His freedom from the enslavement of worldly power, money, status, self-pride and self-reliance. *Whoever boasts should boast in the Lord (2 Cor. 11:17).* Let Jesus be our boast and ideal.

In the simplicity and purity of your life, Lord, we take our refuge within to experience and boast of the power of your freedom. Help us to overcome illusive temptations that detract us from yourself and your call to holiness.

---

9   Mother Teresa of Calcutta, Jesus the Word to be Spoken, Servant Books, Ann Arbor MI, 1986

Enlarging the Face of Christ Amongst Us

We are called to honor the Christ in our brothers and sisters for they are endowed with unique and diverse gifts. This diversity is in itself a gift for it serves to complement and build up the entire body of Christ on earth (cf. Rom 12:4-8). With and in Christ we struggle through and with the diversity in order to celebrate it. The differences are often glaring and sometimes painful as the myriad of personalities and gifts are displayed before us. Yet these very differences have a vital place in the mosaic needed to enlarge and display the holy face of Christ in the world. A portrait of the lives of the saints shows this to us. The sharp and different edges do complement each other and fit, if we allow the Holy Spirit to bring them together into a perfect fit that preserves the beauty and worth of each individual piece while at the same time expanding the overall portrait of the Living Christ.

It is a difficult and sometimes painful skill and spiritual discipline to develop. It takes practice strengthened by a willing spirit and the gift of grace. As we better recognize and interpret the differences, we can better see and appreciate the fullness of Christ's life amongst us.

We are not called to judge the individual pieces. But we are called to recognize, appreciate and embellish the pieces that make up His body and face amongst us. There is a place for each of us. And the kingdom and will of God would not be complete without each and every one of us.

Help us Lord to honor and celebrate the uniqueness you have given to others and us in portraying your holy presence. The diversity is a gift that serves to embellish, strengthen and expand all of us. In our diversity we find our true oneness. And in our oneness is found your glorious diversity. We praise and thank you for this wonder.

Peace: the Gift, Guide and Measure

The gift of peace is a gift of the Risen Christ. In receiving it, we are called to abide in it. It is meant to govern our thoughts, actions and reflections. Because it is of God and His will, it is the most vital and pertinent measure. Thus there is constant need to be sensitive to the presence or absence of peace, and to what brings or takes away its presence. To be an instrument of peace was the prayer and goal of St. Francis Assisi. We share this need and prayer. Peace comforts and refreshes us. It also fuels us to be a comfort and source of renewal to others as we move about our daily lives. In being affirmed by God's peace, there is also the need to affirm others; to love, accept and share with them as we are loved, accepted and share in the life of Christ's peace. In doing so all of us are healed and brought more fully into the Life of Christ.

Let the peace of Christ control your hearts (Col 3:15). Let us be aware of and sensitive to the peace that must rule our hearts and direct our feet. Peace is God's gift and affirmation that we are doing His will and being His people in all things. His peace will surely not be with us if we are not doing the right and good thing. As we enter the right place and good thing, His peace affirms and confirms it. God's will and peace go together. In God's will we find holiness and righteousness that produces peace because it is peace.

It is for us to have the courage and wisdom to take the walk of peace always. The absence of inner peace should serve to propel us away from the places and things that are not in accord with God's will. Conversely the gift of peace will affirm the right places and things. It is for us to walk in it simply and purely, and always with a grateful and childlike heart. God is love. God is peace. We must not run from this. Rather we must run toward and in it. Let the peace reign within. Let there be a vision of peace made possible by a heart that rests in God. This peace is participation in the divine life, a communion with God's will, preference and desire for us. It makes us holy by making us lovers of God, self and neighbor. *My peace I give to you*, our Lord tells us (Jn 14:27). Abide in it. This grace is precious. Keep it close, but lightly and dependently. It belongs to God. It belongs to us only when we belong to Him and we are made one with Him in His peace. In this peace we have holiness and the power to serve God as He wills it. Our intention and activity must be rooted in Christ. It must be grace-filled to be truly efficacious. It must come from and be directed toward Christ Jesus who is grace upon grace (cf. Jn 1:16).

Rely on the mighty Lord; constantly seek his face (Ps. 105:4). Contact with the living God enables us to move in His way and will as we say *yes* to His peace. Enthusiasm, which is the affirmation of God's will and grace, sustains us in the right direction and place. This enthusiasm and peace are real. It is the real thing, genuine not illusionary or fraudulent. It is practical in its everyday realization. It is fundamental and essential.

In humble obedience to the duties and circumstances of daily life we find God's will and give our loving response to God's great love. God gives His peace to feed, precede and lead us, so that we may feed and lead others in His way, life and truth. The gift and opportunity are truly precious.

In being affirmed by God's peace, we are strengthened. But what is given is not just for enjoyment. It is particularly meant for employment in Our Lord's vineyard. The strength of affirmation becomes enthusiasm for what it is that the Lord calls us to be and do. Genuine enthusiasm for some-thing is affirmation of God's will, assuming of course that it is something good and moral. It is a way of Our Lord saying, "Go for it...Be there...Serve here...I am with you!" The affirmation leads to enthusiasm that leads back to affirmation. And the cycle continues: Being fed to feed others so that they and we are fed. What I do for myself in the Spirit, I do for others. What I do for others in the Spirit, I do for myself. One becomes the other. It is one. We are one. But only in Christ Jesus is this so. This can only happen in Christ Jesus who is Lord of all. Jesus is the door through whom we have life. All who enter through Him are saved and *will go in and out and find pasture (Jn 10:9)*. It is for us to learn to listen to the Spirit in stillness and solitude as He speaks to us His enthusiasm in the activity and movements of life.

Spirit of Christ may we be ever more sensitive to your movement within and through us. May we allow your peace to direct and conquer all things, including ourselves.

The Right Connections

It is good to reside in peace. Our Holy Mother Church provides the right connections to accomplish this. These connections include the celebration of our Lord's presence in the liturgy, Scripture, sacraments, prayer, adoration, spiritual books and direction, Christian fellowship and service. From these we gain a gospel vision of life along with the sacramental and other power needed to walk in communion with the saints on earth and in heaven. The peace generated within mixes with the swirling, unsettled world around us. And we simultaneously experience both the crucified, struggling Christ and the risen, victorious Christ.

Worldly vision, attitudes and pursuits push aside Christ and His Church that connect man with God. The cornerstone is rejected (cf. Mt 21:42). Religion *per se* is not invited or welcomed in the design, construct, or display of many or most civil policies and pursuits. Yet when suited to political gain, eloquence or purpose, religious language and identi-fication are employed. But it is usually temporary employment. It ends quickly and abruptly. Prayer becomes a troublesome public activity that usually brings about legal actions rather than the reform and transformation intended and needed. However in our pockets we carry coinage that says *In God We Trust*. A profound contradiction?

When Jesus, the wisdom of God, became incarnate the world changed forever. It became connected again with God through divine means. The gate was opened for the world to renew itself in the image of God. Its model and means was and is Christ. The invitation and means endure. Some respond. Others ignore and deny. With Paul we need to hear again: *Do not be afraid... I am with you (Acts 18:9-10)*. With God and His church there is hope. In this hope and trust we find enduring peace and power. To render to Caesar is not enough. Neither is it the first priority. When we render to God what is His, we get peace. Then we can render to Caesar a vision that is connected to God. Then God's will is done and peace established. Otherwise a vital piece of the grand mosaic, a vital peace, will be missing. And the brokenness will continue. It is for us to make the right connections.

Jesus and His Church are one. They are inseparable. We cannot have Jesus without His Church. Nor can we have the Church without Jesus. As the Blessed Mother Mary gave birth to the Incarnate Jesus, Our Holy Mother Church gives spiritual birth to the Crucified but Risen Jesus into the world. Our Holy Mother Mary and Church teach and point us to Jesus. That is their mission. Through the power of the Holy Spirit the way, life and truth of Jesus are presented and mothered within us. What is presented and modeled for us through the Church is not the same "god" that the secular-minded present to us in the marketplace. The upward mobility mania that permeates the marketplace does not fit the humble walk and posture that Christ followed and shared with the blessed mother. Are we then to sell the Christ revealed in Scripture, religious experience and the lives of the saints for a secular model that runs smoothly and efficiently in the marketplace? Obviously not! But we have to absorb the personal cost of a Christ-centered life. And be open to the spiritual gifts that come in return.

The goals, orientation and language articulated in the marketplace do not fit the teachings that form the Christ. It is for Holy Mother Church endowed with the Holy Spirit to form the Christ within us and to become His living body on earth. In continuing Jesus' mission, we are called to conform our involvement and environment to Christ's standards and way. In living the beatitudes of Christ we free others and ourselves from worldly entrapments that dominate and consume lives, leaving a trail of anxiety and insecurity instead of the abundant life promised and given by Jesus. The abundant life has personal freedom as its inner core and energy, not enslavement. Jesus came to free us, and through His church He offers a way of life that is detached from worldly models of power and status. Our attachment is to the way, life and truth revealed and offered by Christ. In this attachment comes inner freedom from worldly entrapments. We are no longer seduced into pursuing a worldly model of success. Through inner freedom we are made free to serve the best interests of a world that is in vital need of the purity and unselfishness that the Christ life offers. Our call is *to make a straight highway for the Lord (Is 40:3)*. We are to walk according to His word, objectives and goals. It is a walk that Isaiah spoke about and which Jesus made. It is to be a highway undefiled. A sacred way. It is the way of Jesus our Light, Mary, Joseph and all the saints that the Church holds forth as true beacons of God's holy light and Spirit. We are called and invited to freely walk this highway that leads to our heavenly home rather than being seduced by worldly ways and enticements that entrap and diminish our true dignity and inheritance. Our call and dignity is to be brothers and sisters of Christ Jesus. Living in His image, we are to show to the world the fruits of the Good Life. They include love, which brings joy, peace, patience, kindness, faithfulness, gentleness, generosity and chastity (Gal 5:22). It is a love for and in Christ that floods our hearts and spills over to others. Our gift is Jesus who has sent the Paraclete, the Holy Spirit, to dwell within us and embrace us with His love. This gift is particularly entrusted to and presented by His living, visible body on earth, His Holy Church. This Church is holy because Christ is its head. But it is only holy to the extent that it is like Christ. Nevertheless its life is sustained, guided and corrected by the Holy Spirit through all times. And it will endure for all times.

Lord Jesus as church we are your brothers and sisters, made so by your precious blood. May we walk worthy of your gift and sacrifice, closely connected to you and your peace through your church.

Jesus is Newness

Jesus is newness. In His life, teachings and grace we have a new way to see and experience life. *Whoever is in Christ is a new creation; the old things have passed away; behold new things have come (2 Cor 5:17).* In the Spirit of Christ there is newness and freedom. He asks us to drink of this new wine of freedom poured out upon us. We cannot put this new wine into old skins of sinful thought and behavior, it will burst through (cf. Lk 5:36-37).New skins healed of disorder and corrupted forms of behavior are needed to give witness to the new wine received and to carry us to greater holiness. With new lives expanded by the teachings and Spirit of Christ, we will be transformed and room made for His new wine to flow within and through us. In time, the skins will expand to embrace the very image of Our Lord and Master.

When our lives are renewed in Christ, we have more wisdom, more purity, more spiritual vision, more humble obedience to truth and love, and we are better centered. In Christ we find the perfection of virtues and fullness of grace and truth (cf. Jn 1:14). Christ is our ideal. And we should never settle for less, as Blessed Mother Theresa of Calcutta instructed us with her words and example.[10]

Jesus is the leader and perfecter of our faith (Heb 12:2). Now we experience Him as Spirit teaching and leading us within to a deeper faith. He feeds us in sacrament, word, and church, all of which carry the guarantee of the Holy Spirit until the end of time. And He leads us to a deeper realization of His abiding presence within and amongst us, regardless of the circumstances that surround us. One day, the Last Day, we will face Him face-to-face. There will be no further need of question or doubt. We will bask in the vastness of His light and newness. All will be made new in Him (cf. Rv 21:5). Forever and ever new. *We shall bear the image of the heavenly one (1 Cor 15:49).* We shall realize the *culmination* of the communion, celebration and presence that we now experience in the present.

Lord Jesus with and in you we are a new creation that can only make us more, now and forever. In you alone is this newness initiated and then sustained forever. It is truly a life-giving experience that never ends. Our whole life is meant to be a hallelujah.

---

[10] Blessed Mother Theresa of Calcutta, Jesus is the Word to be Spoken, Servant Books, Ann Arbor, MI

The Humble Crown

When we are big enough within, we will be big enough to become little before others. Jesus emptied Himself in humble obedience (cf. Phil 2). So must we, through grace, empty ourselves of self-centered pride and ambition and pour out our lives in humble service to and for others (cf. 1 Pt 5:5). Strengthened within through humility, we can become gentle with others. We can be strong enough to be kind. And when we are strong enough to be kind and gentle, we are most like Jesus who is meek and humble of heart (cf. Mt 11:29). There is no need to play and be "king of the mountain" when the gentle and meek King of kings takes up residence in our hearts.

In the way, life and truth of Christ true kingship is established. Humility is its emblem of honor. In the image and presence of Christ the victory is already won. We can live and walk prayerfully, quietly, peacefully and victor-iously just as the Blessed Mother Mary, her spouse Saint Joseph, and all the saints who have won the crown of eternal life and victory. The crown can only be gained and worn humbly. The worldly-minded neither knows nor believes this. Because God's Spirit is revealed to the little ones (cf. Lk 10:21). Only to the little ones willing to humble themselves before God's wisdom and grace, does the humble Spirit of Christ come and anoint believers with spiritual gifts of His wisdom and peace-filled way.

St. Peter provides eloquent instruction on the humble way to us: *All of you, clothe yourselves with humility in your dealings with one another, for: 'God opposes the proud but bestows favor on the humble.' So, humble yourselves under the mighty hand of God, that he may exalt you in due time. (1 Pet. 5:5-6)*

So it is with and through humility that we turn to God, acknowledging our poverty only to be filled with the richness of His gifts. In doing so, the poor in spirit are truly blessed (cf. Mt 5:3). They are truly happy and at peace within.

Lord may we not let pride rob us of the crowning gift of your humble way. You are the Master we choose to follow because we are chosen to have a share in your holy life. May we better live the gift received.

The Heart and Cross of Jesus

The heart we need is the heart of Jesus. It is meek and gentle (cf. Mt 11:29). Docile and obedient. Kingdom schooled and disciplined. It is a heart that is in love. And it is a heart that is rooted in the community of the Trinity *and* the human community of which my neighbor and I are one and equal. It's a two dimensional and relational love to which we are called. The challenge is to keep them in proper balance. The vertical dimension relates to our Trinitarian love. It is first and foremost. The horizontal dimension relates to our brothers and sisters in this world. One validates the other, energizes the other, and needs the other for us to be a complete and whole person in this world.

We find the portrait of this two-dimensional wholeness in the heart and cross of Jesus, the God-man. He is both priest and victim. His love for the Father and humanity is so great that He is *willing* to die on the cross and suffer for it. And that love is so powerful that it raises the dead and gives us life in the Risen and Victorious Christ. The

Holy Spirit is that love dwelling in our hearts, making us one with and in the heart of Jesus (cf. Rom 5:5). Rooted and built up in Christ through the Holy Spirit (cf. Col 2:6-7), we are empowered with the fruits of the Spirit and are able to walk with our brothers and sisters in *love, joy, peace, patience, gentleness, generosity, kindness, faithfulness and chastity (Gal 5:22)*. It is imperative that we first be rooted. Otherwise there can be no fruits. To have a right relationship with our brothers and sisters, we must first have a relationship with our God and Savior. The cross embodies both dimensions of the love relationship needed to be whole.

The vertical dimension points us to our heavenly Father. While the horizontal dimension stretches out to all our brothers and sisters, embracing them with the love of and for the Father. We cannot choose one to the exclusion of the other. To negate one is to negate the other. *If we say that we love God and hate our brother we are liars (1 Jn 4:20)*. And we can have no part in the kingdom of God. It is no easy matter to love our brothers and sisters in all situations. Neither is it easy to love God at all times, especially when things are not going well. On a purely human plane, it is outright impossible to do either at all times. *But with God nothing is impossible (Lk 1:37)*. Living this love of God and humanity involves struggle, sacrifice and other aspects of the cross. Jesus invites us to share in His redemptive way by accepting and participating in this love for God and man. He invites us to share in His cross and to receive the power of His love in our hearts. In accepting, we become one with the heart and cross of Jesus. We share in the reality and power of Jesus' love for the Father and all His creatures. With St. Paul we pray: *To be strengthened with power through his Spirit in the inner self, that Christ may dwell in our hearts through faith; that rooted and grounded in love we may have strength to comprehend with the holy ones what is the breadth and length and height and depth of the love of Christ that surpasses knowledge (Eph 3:16-19).* Our call is to love with all our strength. The more we love the stronger we become. The stronger we become the more we love. We love because we love. And the way to love is to be rooted in the way and love of Jesus.

Lord God your love knows no boundaries. But it intersects in the holy cross and person of Christ Jesus. Strengthen us within with the love of Christ and His holy cross.

Partnering with Christ Jesus

To partner with Christ, we must first learn to listen to Him within us, and for Him through the people and circum-stances we encounter. But the voice heard silently and deeply within must be the same voice we hear and recognize speaking to our hearts through the people and circumstances encountered in our daily life. Words and circumstances in and of themselves are not sufficient. They must touch hearts that have first been opened and made loving by our Lord's silent, active voice within. We must first come to recognize the Shepherd's gentle, inviting, caring and faithful voice within our hearts before we can hear and respond to His voice speaking to us through the people and circumstances in our lives. What we really come to recognize is the Heart of Jesus speaking to our hearts — the Spirit of Jesus speaking to our spirit. "Say what you will, the tongue speaks just to the ears. But the heart speaks to the heart," St. Francis de Sales reminds us.

I will draw them into the desert and there speak to their hearts (Hos 2:16). To speak to our hearts our Lord, by example and invite, draws us into the desert of solitude and silence. In the silence and solitude there are no other people, activity or distractions. There is only God and the tempter. Our free choice of God draws us deep within our hearts where our Lord faithfully awaits us and where the tempter cannot go because only love can go there.

Our open surrender to God deeply within enables Him to weed out the falseness and allow His truth-filled presence to make our wounded hearts whole and healthy again. The stale air of past mistakes is swept away. The fresh, pure air of freedom is breathed into us so that we may once again worship our Holy Lord and He alone in our hearts. Our unconditional surrender to God, through the teachings and person of Jesus, assures God's abiding presence. He has promised that if we hold fast to His teachings in faith, He and the Father will make their home in us (cf. Jn 14:23). Jesus does not lie. He is only truth and fulfillment.

Through the cleansing of solitude and silence, we begin to hear and live in accordance with truth – the truth about our real self that is rooted in God who is truth. God endures falseness. But He neither invites, courts nor ever marries it. Rather He waits until we are freely willing to put aside our false selves and embrace our true selves found in God alone. In the embrace of truth, we find and experience freedom. *The truth will set you free (Jn 8:32).* We are free to be honest about ourselves and acknowledge our total dependence upon God. We gain a true sense of our poverty but only to realize the richness that God bestows upon us in doing so. Without God, who is love (cf. 1 Jn

4:8), we are nothing (cf. 1 Cor 13). Without God we have nothing lasting to offer. We can only offer temporal success and recognition that will pass in and with time. Not a very wise choice in the face of eternity! But God's words, which are spirit and life (cf. Jn 6:63), shall never pass away (cf. Lk 21:33).

It is for us to keep choosing the Word of God, Jesus Christ, and all that He has said to us. In this we have eternal life. It is a wise choice indeed.

In choosing to partner with you Lord Jesus we are joined with truth, freedom and life eternal. And we are made real, whole and one, now and forever. Help us to keep choosing you at all times and in all circumstances that our lives may rest in you and your holy oneness.

Our Master's Voice

In the fullness of time we received Jesus, the gift of the Father, into the world. Through baptism and faith we have received the gift of the Holy Spirit, who makes us one with and in Christ. Through the action of the Holy Spirit within us, we are able to experience our Lord's risen and glorified life, and His victory over the darkness of sin and death in our lives. In this gift of the Spirit we come to know His voice and presence within us. It is a gentle voice, simple and pure. Like the Master's voice, our lives must become gentle, simple and pure. This is largely accomplished through openness and surrendering to our Lord's call and voice (Latin *voce*) as we consent to His presence within us and within our lives. It is a simple and pure *yes* to all that He sends or allows to happen to us.

Through unconditional surrender to His presence within us, we can listen attentively and deeply to Him in each person and situation. We do not attempt to control. On the contrary, we open ourselves to the Christ within us and within our lives by letting go of control. It is an unconditional surrender. Through surrender to God within us we become attached to Him alone and thus detached from all other control. In letting go, we allow God to act in all situations. In acknowledging His presence and providence, we receive the grace to celebrate His glory regardless of the flavor of the situation, hard or pleasant. God's love is unconditional. So must our surrender to His presence through all things and places be unconditional.

There is nothing to fear. He calls in love. We answer in love. There is nothing that can separate us from His love (cf. Rom 8:38-39), even if we should temporarily fail to love Him in return. His call of love and to love is unconditional and unending. We are invited to become this unconditional love, and live the abundant life in the unending kingdom of God, who is love. Jesus is the door and the Holy Spirit is the key that opens the door to the life of love in Our Father's House. But we have to say *yes*, again and again, to the home being built in our hearts by the Blessed Trinity. We must choose to reside in this love. With and through this loving heart, we can listen to His presence and experience His peace. It is so simple and gifted that there is a temptation to flee, fight or deny it! But the gentle, sure voice tells us, *remain in me as I remain in you (Jn 15:4)*.

Lord your voice resonates with gentleness and love. May it resound in all our life experiences and choices. May we not let a clamorous world drown out the gentle purity of your loving voice and call within us.

Walking the Road of Holiness

To remain in Christ demands that we walk the road of holiness, for He is holy. But this road of holiness is built stone by stone, foot by foot, moment by moment. It is a daily construct that requires God's grace and our response. Little by little we grow along what John Cassian calls *the level road of perfection.*[11] It seems imperceptible at first. Yet we reflect for a moment to realize, for instance, that we have become less disturbed, angry, defensive or egocentric in our behavior and relationships. We gradually begin to better see God's grace in our lives and the lives of others, and come to better realize that the road of holiness and peace is being built within us and around us.

Our lips and actions begin to be better synchronized with the love in our hearts. Warmth is generated. Though small and seemingly imperceptible, a new reality is being created. It is of the kingdom of justice, joy and peace in the Holy Spirit (cf. Rom 14:17). Humble and kind

---

[11] John Cassian: The Conferences, Ancient Christian Writers, translated by Boniface Ramsey, O.P. Newman Press, N.Y. 1997

service, reconciliation, harmony, chastity, gentleness and faithfulness mark the road of holiness. And we better realize that there is no other way that leads to our everlasting home. But we stumble. The weight of our sins and the sins around us mixed with discouragement draws us to the ground. So we look to Jesus carrying all our sins on the cross and his falling to the ground three times in exhaustion. But He got up and kept walking right to his death and glorification. And so must we keep getting up, each time with greater commitment and realization that like Jesus it all ends in victory, not defeat, and a risen life that is everlasting. Such is our way and heritage.

It is not so much a matter of *getting there* as it is a matter of *being here*. What we are doing now and here will get us there if we just persist and keep walking with Jesus. It is for us to do our best and leave the rest to God. He will get us there. To do so, we need to keep hearing and accepting divine wisdom: *Trust God and God will help you; and he will direct your way (Sir 2:6)*. Our work is to stay on the road and to love in His name. We need to be disciplined, faithful, consistent and trusting. We also need to be humble and flexible enough to receive correction as the road of life curves and bends with various relationships and events. However the road travels, the love, forgiveness and peace of Christ are always there to heal and strengthen us if we are open to His embrace and obedient to His ways. In the simple, quiet acceptance of His presence, we are gifted and kept on the simple path of holiness. In this holiness we are healed and made whole. In our healing, we become healing to others. In receiving the Holy Spirit we are able to give what we have received to others. In receiving love we become love. It is an inclusive and living love that is spoken to others in many ways and words. It is meant for them as it is meant for us. We are called to be the forgiveness that God is breathing into us. To be the love that He is in our heart. To be the peace that He speaks to our heart. Not to be this is not to be our true self, and not to be of God. Anything else coming out of us is not of God. It is false. Our call is to worship and serve God in spirit and truth (cf. Jn 4:24). To do less, is to be less.

The road to holiness leads to more, never less. Lord, Jesus, help us to keep getting up and not lose heart or be less than you desire and call us to be.

Christ is the Vision, Portrait and Focus

Christ is the vision, portrait and focus. It is He who is our model, life and truth in all that we do. He is central to all of it. Focused on the Master's teachings and life, we receive the grace of His Spirit. The Holy Spirit enables us to become like Him, and to position ourselves to share in His divinity through the humanity He has already consecrated by His coming. Christ is it! There is no other name, no other one through whom we are saved and brought home (cf. Acts 4:12). The Christ style of life is to be ours. Humble, gentle, simple, obedient, loving, serving...all the marks of Christ are to be ours as well for we are His brothers and sisters. They will often bring persecution, ridicule and rejection. The Master guarantees this by his example and teachings (cf. Jn 15:20). They will also make visible to others the Christ, humble and meek of heart. So we are not to despair or be afraid. The road is simple and level. But it certainly is not easy to travel.

SPIRIT OF CHRIST

Many will mock the foolishness that is seen in the flesh through secular eyes. However, Jesus walked it. So did Mary, Joseph, and the multitude of saints over the past 2000 years. A holy life is a Christ-centered life. His Spirit has been poured forth upon the earth. It is for us to receive and repeat God's gift to one another. A holy life brings victory, now and in the world to come. A Christ-centered life is a lived success and triumph, now and always.

More than *doing* for Christ, we must *be* in Christ. For if we are not in Christ, prayerfully and dutifully grafted to life with Him, we will not be able to do lasting and valued things that give life to other branches. A modern slogan says, "Just do it!" However the contemplative spiritual masters counsel us to "Just be!" Just be in Christ and *then* we can do it simply, humbly and effectively. That is to say, be in Christ through the indwelling Spirit and let this abundance spill over to our neighbor in good and loving deeds and words.

To be in Christ Jesus, we must be alert and sober (cf. 1 Thes 5:6). We must be attentive to God's presence and authority. Emotions, peer pressure, human acceptance and acclaim, immediate gratification, political correctness and many other forces would pull us off the road of holiness. Yet if we simply surrender to Christ and not to the deceptions, Christ does become the only source of strength, truth and wisdom leading us to the real and abundant life. To be in Christ, we are invited to receive Him in Eucharist and become His gift to others. St. Therese of Lisieux tells us, "We are also Hosts which Jesus wants to change into

Himself."[12] To be in Christ we must pray, and from this prayer base serve others in His Name. To be in Christ, we must receive Him in word and worship Him at His altar until we stand before the fullness of His throne in heaven. All of this is gift to the *chosen few* who have *chosen* to receive and believe in order to re-live the Christ in their lives. Our worship begins on earth but its culmination is in heaven. This also is true of the sacred matters of prayer, Eucharist, word and healing.

In prayer we are changed and healed. The culmination of the changes and healing is fully realized in heaven where we will be like Him: holy, pure and joy-filled. We go to prayer to be changed and healed. If you do not want to change or be healed, then do not pray. In praying, we become changed and healed in visible and invisible ways so that others can become changed and healed in Christ. In receiving and believing in God's love for us, we can become God's love to others. In becoming the beloved, we allow ourselves to become love to others and enable them to be loved in the right and only true way: In Christ. It is in and through the Spirit of Christ, Crucified and Risen, that we are able to see and experience things differently. We are able to have a Christ-centered spirituality that will *not* allow us to do secular things that are profitable in the accepted ways of the world yet may offend God. Rather we are moved to invest our talents, time and resources in the small, needy, weak and outcast members of our society who are in real need. They are the least in the eyes of the

---

12   St. Therese Lisieux, Poem

world yet they are the favored ones in Christ and thus very precious. A different measure is used to have a different pleasure. The pleasure is in serving Christ Himself who is found in the least i.e., those who are in need. And the yield, we learn in the Gospel of Matthew, is everlasting when it is done in Christ and for Christ (cf. Mt 25:34-40). The small actually make us great rather than the great making us small in God's way and sight. Only the way, life and truth of Christ can empower us to see and better live this vision.

Lord Jesus may we see with your eyes, perceive with your mind, and love with your heart. May we keep doing it until we see you face-to-face in heaven.

The Holy Spirit Must Act

It is the Holy Spirit who must act within our hearts and through our lives, making us innocent as children and straight-forward reflections of God's light. It is the person and teachings of Christ that we hold forth to share before the world (cf. Phil 2:16). We surrender to Jesus who is the light in order to become His light through the indwelling Spirit. The surrender within allows the Holy Spirit to circumcise our worldly hearts and minds, cutting away the pride and arrogance in order to place our skills and abilities before God's grace and use. A right order is in order: First God and His grace, then what we add will be used rightly. In actions and prayer, we must let God do His thing. We must not get in His way. He must act so that we may act rightly. He can write straight with the crooked lines of our mistakes. We must let Him act and lead, and give Him time to do so. Being patient with God and our self is a requisite. A priest-friend kept a pertinent poster prominently displayed in his office as a reminder to himself and others. It simply said: "Be patient. God is not through with me yet!"

There is no need to get discouraged, complain or grumble if we believe strongly that God is at work to make things right with our collaboration. He will do it. We must walk humbly but confidently with Him. It is not necessary to understand. But it is necessary to trust. We may not even understand the results, and wonder how God has moved us from there to here. But the peace and calm in the "new here" emanates from and is sustained by trust.

We simply trust in the Good Shepherd for we are His sheep and listen for His voice. If we live this faith, He will lead us beside the gentle waters in the green pastures of His peace. And there is nothing to fear (cf. Ps 23).

I was stupid and could not understand; I was a brute beast in your presence. Yet I am always with you; you take hold of my right hand. With your counsel you guide me, and at the end receive me with honor (Ps 73:22-24).

Holy Lord may the sunshine of child-like trust and the warmth of your gentle presence remove all fear in our lives. May we freely and patiently allow you to lead us to abundant life.

The Oil of Gladness

In our busy lives we need the oil of gladness and prayer to make them run properly. Both are gifts of the Holy Spirit. As we look upon our world, discouragement and dismay abound in the midst of global turbulence and unrest. But the Spirit of God, Isaiah tells us, gives us the oil of gladness instead of mourning (cf. Is 61:3). With Peter's successor, the Church enters the third millennium and successive millennia with strong hope, and in doing so we become witnesses to hope as John Paul II so eloquently proclaimed with his words and life during his long and celebrated pontificate. While a quick perusal of world events sends up clouds darkened with discouragement, the Holy Spirit within enlightens us with living hope and courage. *We rejoice in our hope of sharing the glory of God… and this hope will not disappoint us, because God's love has been poured forth into our hearts through the Holy Spirit which has been given to us (Rom 5:2-5).* We are gifted with the light of confident hope and victory. There is no room for fear in an interior room that is filled with the living love and hope of the Holy Spirit. God is in residence here. It is He who anoints us with His oil of gladness to make our busy lives run smoothly and evenly in the midst of a tumultuous world. A prayerful posture enables us to experience and celebrate this mysterious victory. This small investment of time and attention in prayer yields such a powerful return! Why do so many souls cling so tenaciously to worldly liabilities when they can be successfully balanced and richly overwhelmed by the assets of the Holy Spirit?

Too often we let our rational minds run away from our loving hearts. Having run away from our true home, we are then free to indulge in endless analyses of the complexities of a broken world and how to best fix them. But it is to this broken world that our Lord's love came to save it from the darkness of discouragement, disillusionment and "disconnectiveness." The saving love of Jesus poured forth on the cross fully displayed just how much God really loves the world (cf. Jn 3:16). He invites us to keep our rational minds connected to the love of God in our hearts. This love is so great that it embraces everyone and clothes him or her with a hope that will not be disappointed. Our call and gift from God is to live gladness not sorrow, victory not defeat, hope not despair, and love not fears. It is fitting that John Paul II's successor, Pope Benedict XVI, issued his first encyclical, *Deus Caritas Est,* God is Love, and published his popular and scholarly book, *Jesus of Nazareth,* to help us better see, know and serve the loving Christ to whom we belong and place our hope.

Holy Lord you gladden our steps and fill our hearts with hope and love to make all the way to heaven a heavenly experience. Let us run to you with hope-filled hearts, never away from you into the darkness of despair. Help us to remember your abiding presence and accessible assistance.

The Way Home

We are all on the way home to God. But it takes an attentive, willing and loving heart to get there and win His eternal presence. It takes a heart that is attuned to the quiet, joyful presence and stirrings of the indwelling Holy Spirit – the heaven that has begun in us. When we are walking in the right direction and attitude there is peace, there is His presence. Otherwise an abiding and deepening dissatisfaction and distaste permeates our experience. In contrast to this the Holy Spirit moves us like the prodigal son toward home and the taste of Goodness. It is God's call to His children to come home. It is His mercy and stirring within us that gets us there. It is for us to pay attention to the good taste, good presence and good home that awaits us if we but turn and walk toward it. In doing so, we have already arrived. That is, we already sense and experience the rightness and the fragrance of the good food and life. Or we can choose to linger in the misery of our false self, wallowing in depression, despair and the pain of being far way from home. A church roadside sign posed this question: "If God seems far away, guess who moved?"

In His unending mercy, Christ calls to our hearts to come home. And every step toward home is an experience of home. It is for us to choose Christ with each step of our lives. Choose life (cf. Jer 21:8-9). He has chosen us sinners to be redeemed, forgiven and sanctified by His holy presence. He wants and invites us to share His home, beginning now.

He also invites us to share His cross as the way to get there. There are no short cuts. There is and will be struggle and suffering. But it is redemptive suffering that is coated with confident triumph not defeat. Christ neither explains nor removes the suffering. He simply fills it with His holy and loving presence, giving us both strength and the assurance of ultimate victory. Thus the cross becomes our glory now and in eternity, as it is His. It is the Spirit of the Father and Son who makes His home in us as we open ourselves and travel the way of Christ toward our eternal home. Humility and repentance open the door to the Great Comforter. Pride closes it. Our dependence is upon God dwelling and moving within us. Like the prodigal son we need to be reminded of home (cf. Lk 15:17). We need to remember. We need to be "*re-membered*" with our true home. In this remembering we turn to Him and He in turn runs to greet us.

St. Paul reminds us to *think of what is above (Col. 3:2)*. We have to face the realities of our lives. But face the reality of God above all else! That is, come to the reality of God's closeness and friendship. Be conscious through prayer-filled living of His immanence. Be also aware of His transcen-dence that goes way beyond us and is way above us. He is both intimately close and powerfully beyond us. That is what makes Him God! Jesus is our Risen Lord and friend. He walks with us. He doesn't have to prove Himself to us. It has all been said by His cross and risen life. We are called to simply accept and experience the grace of it. Be open to it. Dwell in it. Let its freshness and dynamism embrace us. Let God be God, purely and simply. He is not waiting for us to do something spectacular or special to be worthy of His presence.

He is already present and active. Acknowledge it in faith. Walk in it in reality. Let us be humble enough to let Him act. He moves all things including you and me. Let us be grateful for the many ways in which He enters our hearts, moves our feet, and carries us to wholeness.

Let us be more aware of whom He sends to assist us, and to whom we are sent to assist. We live in relationship, a relationship to God within us and around us in others. It is His presence that must be the center of it all, not ours. It is for us to listen for what He is saying and trying to do for us, to us, through us, and with us. If it conforms to the teachings and image of Christ, it is right. Otherwise beware of who is speaking and influencing us. There are other voices seeking a relationship with us that do not have Christ as the beginning, center, means and end. It is for us to listen with our hearts to the heart of Jesus as His love and Spirit resonates within and around us.

Lord Jesus in your humanity the reality of divinity was made known. May it be your voice and Spirit that resounds in our humanity. May it be your presence that is made known. May it be your Spirit that shows us the way home and strengthens us along the way.

The Gift and Reality of Love

There are many ways of seeing and experiencing Christ. But they all have a common ingredient: Love. Unconditional love and goodness belong to Him. And St. John of the Cross reminds us "Nothing is obtained from God except by love."[13] It is for us to choose to receive the gift of love in each moment, to rest in it and become love. Abbot William of St. Thierry, *On the Contemplation of God*, teaches us that our salvation consists of receiving from God the gift of loving Him and being loved by Him. He further tells us that we cannot be what we are created to be except by loving God. In being open to God's merciful love, His will can be done in us as we love Him in return. We can be healed of broken relationships. Barriers to God's presence and way can be removed. Sin, the absence of God and thus absence of Love, can be overcome. We cannot earn this love and goodness. It is a gift to receive and respond to. By His love we are made worthy. In our thankfulness

---

13   St. John of Cross, "The Spiritual Canticle", The Collected Works of St. John of the Cross, Kavanaugh & Rodriquez, ICS Publications, 1979.

His love is returned. He is Savior. We are the saved. The question is not, "Is He gracing us in this moment?" Rather it should be: "How is He gracing us in this moment? And how, Lord, can we best let you be Lord?" It is for us also to realize that this is part of a process. It is not done all at once. It is incremental. It must be pondered. But through it all, care is needed not to grieve the Holy Spirit. That is to say, we need to maintain a loving and responsive heart. The unconditional love deserves an unconditional response. A proud, cold heart will not do.

The Good News is intended for the poor, the simple ones who are open to gift. The proud, who neither seek nor sense the need of gifts, have no place or time in their lives for this mystery of Gift. Children love to receive gifts. They love the mystery of a gift package no matter how it is wrapped. Jesus tells us to be like children in receiving the gift of kingdom life in the Spirit that makes us one with and in Him. We are not required to expect, deserve or perhaps even understand the gift. Just receive it through a heart opened by gratitude. May neither arrogance nor exalted expectations shun the gift sent, nor "maturity" diminish the delight of the simple giftedness of God's loving presence regardless of how He decides to package it within the circumstances of our life. God gives. We receive and share. Thus all receive. The Spirit-Gift is meant to be shared. It is only kept by giving it away. The more we give the more we have. The more we receive the more capacity we have to receive and share. We do not possess it, only experience and share it. It is received and sustained only with open hands. If we offer arrogant and possessive fists it can no longer be received. We are no longer open to others and now are only a threat instead of a treat. The door of the kingdom is opened by the humility of child-like trust. It is kept open by receptivity, docility and generosity.

Lord God you are love. In receiving you we become love. In becoming love, others are gifted as well. May we better celebrate the gift of your love in our daily lives, and in doing so give you greater honor and glory.

Called to be Loved

We are called to be loved, a beloved of Christ. The Apostle John teaches us how to be the beloved one of the Lord. After putting aside his high-ranking ambition and becoming schooled in the humble way of Christ, John stayed very close to our Lord Jesus. He learned how to rest his ambitious mind and will on the humble heart and peace-filled breast of our Lord. He leaned on our Lord's presence. He listened to the heart of Jesus. It spoke to John of the warmth of everlasting love and deep friendship beyond understanding. John simply stayed close to the Lord always. This intimacy extended to being a witness at our Lord's transfiguration, death on the cross, and resurrection experience. The gift of always staying close to our Lord was further rewarded when Jesus entrusted His blessed mother Mary to John from the cross. John received the gift of our Blessed Mother's residence with him and truly became her son. What belongs to Mary belongs to God. She knows how to mother the Christ. In welcoming the Blessed Mother to live and walk with us, the Christ is mothered and made incarnate within us. And so it was for John. His closeness to our Lord Jesus was made firm by his being close to our Blessed Mother. In this love, John rested and nurtured his contemplative posture. From it would come his contempla-tive gospel. Love became the essence of his homilies. In his last years when asked to address the disciples, it is said that he would only say, "Love one another as our Lord has loved us." They would ask if there was anything else he could or would say. His response was, "It is enough!"

It is enough for us to stay close to our Lord and receive His love. In doing so, we are moved to give that love to others. And in loving others, our Lord's love is made complete. It is enough to be loved by God and to love Him in our hearts and in our neighbors.

Lord Jesus may we always have the desire, humility and wisdom to stay close to you and realize that our Blessed Mother Mary is our best teacher and intercessor in accomplishing this. With the apostle St. John, may we also realize that we are your beloved disciples.

A Tighter Grip

Our stumbling in life can and should lead us to a tighter grip on Christ, a greater commitment to walk more closely with and in Him. It is not the stumbling that matters. Rather it is the getting up that really matters. The stumbling should serve to make us ever more aware of our weakness and vulnerability. This awareness in turn should stimulate us to get a greater grip on the hand of Christ and to look more intensely upon Him as we better realize our dependence upon Him. The way of the cross includes stumbling. It may be enough that we continue to stumble so that God can show to all His power to pick us up and keep us going. Life is up and down, straight and around, light and darkness. Regard-less, our work is to just cling with child-like trust to Christ through prayer, Eucharist, worship, community and service. It will come out right because it is the right way to walk. Just keep walking. Let the life, way and truth of Jesus transform others and us. It is a victory march when we grip His holy hand. It is despair when we focus on our stumbling rather than the getting up again with faith, hope and love in hand. Each getting up again brings us to a closer and stronger walk with Christ. Jesus believes in each of us or He would never have created us. We must believe in Him and His gifts of faith, hope, and love. Let us keep gripping His hand ever more tightly. He is sufficient.

Lord with you in hand all is in hand. Let us not get discouraged when we slip away from you. Rather let us better know the consequences so that we may turn again ever more quickly to grasp your firm hand and abide with you.

The Talent to Remain in Christ

Our preeminent talent is to remain in Christ through the Holy Spirit who enables us to walk prayerfully in His way. Through the grace-filled work of prayer our walk becomes Christ-centered, with no opposition or division intended between our walk and prayer. Our walk and prayer are meant to become one in Christ. They are two sides of the same coin. The contemplative must roll with the active side, providing the world with the only currency that really matters: the Lordship and authority of Christ Jesus in all things and places. The marketplace of the active life is where our interior beliefs, understanding and principles are tested, affirmed or put aside. It is for us to move from prayer to life and life to prayer. They roll along together. They influence one another, for better or worst. Our prayer should sanctify our active life and our active life should become sacred ground where prayer is lived and celebrated continually. In doing so, there is harmony with the Holy Spirit. It is not necessary to understand all

SPIRIT OF CHRIST

of it. But it is necessary for us to acknowledge, accept and strive to live a prayer-filled active life.

Jesus is Lord. And He draws all things to Himself. He makes them right. Acknowledge and accept Him in all things, at all times, in all places. He who dwells within us in faith dwells amongst us in fact. God's presence is in the present, and we must always be mindful of this. We must acknowledge and reverence Him in what we do, say and think. He is worthy of our love and reverence, not our offenses. It is for us to worship and serve Him with our thoughts, words and actions as we strive to have them flow together prayerfully. It is the Spirit's work to initiate it and our cooperative and collaborative work to complete it. It will happen if we walk hand in hand with Him. But it will take time for our mind and heart, hands and feet to be in harmony with His. He is patient with us. May we also be patient with ourselves. The talent is there for the asking. But it must be accepted and exercised to be made perfect. This takes time, effort and especially grace.

To be and act in God's presence is our call, constant goal, and struggle. Attentiveness and sensitivity to the movement of the Spirit in our prayer and active life are required. One should feed the other and be centered in Christ. Through persistence and grace we strive to balance our resting and our acting in God's presence. There will be no opposition between our contemplative and active life if we persevere in prayer. We are called to both. Prayer will always be the "better part" and priority in our lives. But one should serve and strengthen the other until they truly become one. The trustful resting that enables us to "float" in God's presence should not oppose the Spirit-current's movement. One is dependent upon the other for they flow from the same source of God's goodness, care and abiding presence.

The doing and acting in God's presence serves and strengthens our being and resting in His presence. The converse is equally true. It should all become an act and prayer of holy presence. The monastic life best portrays this. But each of us called to holiness in Christ is meant to live this wherever we are.

In the monastic life, we see communities living a Christ-centered and transformed life. But each of us is called to be transformed as well and become an agent of transformation to the society in which we have been placed. Because we are seldom surrounded by like-minded friends of Christ, the need for an intense and constant prayer life is heightened. The secular minded would have us abandon prayer and become totally immersed in worldly affairs. In doing so, drowning occurs quickly. Only Christ can rescue us from such a fate for there is no other name or way by which we are saved (cf. Acts 4:12).

It is for us to receive the love, peace and wisdom of Christ in simple, humble and constant prayer. And to let it flow in simple, humble loving acts. We must not allow our acts to betray our prayer. It is for us to *trust in the Lord and do good (Ps 3 7:3)* Let it be known in loving acts stemming from the love received. Let us become a loving prayer offered to a troubled and chaotic world that thirsts for justice, peace and joy: the Holy Spirit and kingdom life. Become and give the love freely received. Jesus is our ideal

SPIRIT OF CHRIST

and goal. He is also our Authentic Reality. It is enough for a disciple to become like his teacher: prayerful, joyful, compassionate, single-minded, unselfish, prophetic and mystical, priest and victim, contemplative and active. In Jesus there was and is no opposition between human and divine, contemplative and active. They flow together in perfect harmony. In Jesus we have the model and reality of what perfect humanity is all about as well as the means of striving for it.

God's plans for us are peace not disaster with a future full of hope (cf. Jer 29:11). But we are to seek Him with all our hearts in all situations, times and circumstances (cf. Jer 29:14).

So let us rejoice in Our Lord's indwelling presence, be patient in all things and pray always (cf. Rom 12:12). We cannot walk in two different directions. It is for us to walk in Christ for life is Christ (cf. Phil 1:21). Jesus is Lord of all times, places, things and persons. It is for us to allow Christ to live prayerfully within and amongst us, becoming His eyes and ears, mind, voice, heart, hands and feet in the world that He has already redeemed with His cross and raised with His resurrection. We share the mystery and power of His paschal suffering and risen life. Let us acknowledge not ignore Him in all things so that He may act in and through us and make straight our path (cf. Prv 3:6). With St. John and His church we can proclaim, "It is the Lord!" (John 21:7). At all times, in all places, let us reverence Him with holy lives and walk with prayer-filled grateful hearts.

Lord Jesus, only through a prayer-filled life can we have true unity and meaning in our lives. May prayer feed our active lives and our active lives confirm our prayer life rooted in you. With you, in you, and through you may we neither invite nor show any opposition between our human and divine, active or prayerful sides. Help us to remain one with you, now and forever.

Moving Prayerfully in Heart

Our life of prayer is lived in an attitude of gratitude. It is for us to receive God's grace and thus always be grateful. But we are also called to move in it. It takes prayer-filled discipline to receive and move in God's gift of grace. It also takes a deep discernment in which our heart is the most valuable compass. It is there that we let God alone speak to us directly through His inspirations. We follow a God of love who offers us His peace. "Let this peace of Christ control your hearts," St Paul tells us (Col 3:15). This peace is the measure of His will for us.

As St. Augustine instructs us, we are restless until our hearts rest in Him. But when our hearts turn to rest in Him we are in peace, regardless of the circumstances. To know God within our hearts, our inmost being, is to know peace. But if there is no God there is no peace. Though we walk in His sight, our hearts may not yet be one with His. Our hearts may be too crowded with other things and there is no place for Him in the Inn. He is kept waiting outside. Though His love abides it has not been allowed to penetrate the depths of our heart. When it does, a deep reality of His presence comes and the peace that surpasses understanding embraces us (cf. Phil 4:7). Our heart has come to rest in Him and He alone. Our challenge is to guard our hearts through prayer-filled living so that circumstances or others do not rob us of this peace. Our Lord says, "Peace I leave with you; my peace I give to you. Not as the world gives do I give to you." (Jn 14:27).

We only find peace when our hearts are rooted in Christ. It is for us to receive this holy peace and move in it. We do it gratefully, attentively and always prayerfully. With St. Paul we pray to Our Father to be strengthened with power through his Spirit in the inner self that Christ may dwell in our hearts through faith (cf. Eph 3:16-17).

Lord Jesus you are our peace. In accepting and loving you at all times, we have the power to live holy, prayer-filled lives rooted in you. Without you we are but a shell that awaits the development and growth of the precious pearl that gives us real and enduring worth. In and with you we live and move in an everlasting way.

Must Surrender to Conquer

When we surrender and say *yes* to God within and to all that is happening to us, the Holy Spirit takes control and confers a peace, harmony, strength and quiet confidence to what we are doing and experiencing. The center of control moves from self to God, and we live and move in the Spirit. *The Lord is the Spirit and where the Spirit of the Lord is there is freedom (2 Cor 3:17).* This freedom of the Holy Spirit brings victory over the slavery of self-centeredness and self-imposed controls. In saying *yes* to God we give Him permission to act within us and amongst us. *Commit your way to the Lord; trust that God will act (Ps 37:5).* We give up the illusions of control in our life in order to gain the reality of God's loving power.

God is in the business of doing great things. Heed the Living Guide within who affirms with His peace and moves with His power. It is for us to become obedient to God in His gift of the moment and teaching Spirit with which it is endowed. Let the Holy Spirit direct our thinking, objectives and way as we surrender and conform to God's way, life and truth rather than conforming to the culture in which we are placed. Our call is to be reconciled to Christ. It is He who will reconcile all to Himself (cf. Col 1:20). Sooner or later it will happen, in our time or in eternity.

God sees the whole human race (cf. Ps 33:13). But His eye and focus are especially on those who reverence Him and rely on His love. The Holy Spirit is love, the love of Jesus for the Father and the Father for Jesus. We are invited to say *yes* to the Holy Spirit of love and to become love. When we say *yes* to God's love within, the Holy Spirit of love makes it incarnate within us. Jesus, the love of the Father, is formed in us spiritually as He was made incarnate in the Blessed Mother. The more loving we become the more we image and incarnate Jesus. Our spiritual life is rooted in the love of Jesus, His love for us and our love for Him. Herein is our salvation and redemption. We are called to love God first then all others, including ourselves. Sometimes we forget to love ourselves. As St. Bernard would put it, "For God's sake, love yourself!" Our faith and hope are formed and completed in love. Let us remember what St. John of the Cross teaches us, "Nothing is obtained from God except by love." Without love we are nothing. But with love we conquer all things: *Armor vincit omnia*. Love never fails. It never ends (cf. 1 Cor 13).

Lord Jesus you invite and lead us to surrender. But it is only to claim victory and new life made possible by you. In and through you, we are conquerors. Our only defeat would be to fail to surrender to you and your mighty power. Help us to better claim the victory that you hold and to which you invite us.

Releasing the Power of Jesus' Teachings and Presence

It is true that we experience Jesus within the silence of our inner life. But it is equally true that we experience Him by speaking and releasing the power of His teachings and holy presence. However this proclamation is made possible only through prayerful living, emanating from a deep abiding prayer life. Pope John Paul II reminded us "Jesus was the most prayerful person to walk the earth."[14] Christ's good and vibrant imitation, St. Francis of Assisi, was also a most prayerful person, and so was John Paul II. As followers we are called to this prayerful posture of abiding in God's presence and making this incarnate in our lives. It is difficult to do. But we simply must do it if we are to make a real difference and make known a different way, a different presence, to the worldly-minded. Our call is to put our Lord's prayer life in action and become identified

---

14 Pope John Paul II, Jesus, Son and Savior, Pauline Books, Boston, MA. 1996, p. 413

with His values and ways. He is our companion in life. We are to show that we are His companions as well.

Our love for Christ is demonstrated in the witness we give to His teachings and the compassion extended to others. We are called to: believe what is revealed in Holy Scripture; teach what we believe; and live what we teach. Our experience of Jesus in the Spirit in quiet and communal prayer is to be employed in the vineyard. We are not asked to compromise our prayerful experience and conform ourselves "to this age" (cf. Rom 12:2). Instead we are called to transform this age and culture with the prayer-filled power of God's truth and way. In speaking and living Our Lord's presence and teachings, power and unity with God are experienced within and released to the world around us. If we believe in His teachings, we must also believe and have confidence in His companionship and power in proclaiming and living His teachings. Our command is to go and teach all that He has proclaimed with the assurance that He is with us always (cf. Mt 28:20). We walk and talk on the foundation of God's abiding presence and teachings. Our work on earth is to know and make known God's presence.

There is need to confront the wrong in others and us. But we confront it with God's words and charity. *Do not disdain the discipline of the Lord or lose heart when reproved by him; for whom the Lord loves He disciplines (Heb 12:5-6).* And He loves all of us! Confronting what is wrong in a culture or situation is right. Isaiah was called to this. So was John the Baptist and all the prophets who gave witness to The Prophet, Jesus.

As followers of Jesus we share in His prophetic ministry. Like Blessed Mother Theresa of Calcutta, Thomas Merton and other recent prophets of Christ, we too are called to address the wrongs that mar the face of current humanity. The clarity of vision gained in Scripture, prayer and worship is to be used to boldly address the wrongs that exist in the marketplace and our lives. Boldness stems from holiness. Holiness stems from Jesus given to us in the power of His word, Eucharist, worship, fellowship, reconciliation, hope, praise and promises. "Be perfect," Jesus tells and shows us (Mt 5:48). It implies a constant call and striving to *change* our aim, attitude, speech and thinking until all becomes Christ like.

The power we need and for which the world yearns is found in being holy, being perfect, like Christ. There are no short cuts or easy ways to get there. Only Christ-like holiness will transform our lives and the world in which we live. When we have learned this we will have discovered fire again. *I have come to set the earth on fire and how I wish it were already blazing (Luke 12:49).*

Spirit of Christ, you are the blazing and consuming fire around which we gather to be warmed, then purified, enlightened and empowered with the newness of holiness. Help us to know, experience and make known the power and goodness of your holiness in a world that has grown cold and dark with selfishness and greed. Consume us in the fire of your holiness that we may renew the face and heart of the world.

The Spark of Holiness

The spark of holiness always remains in us through baptism. Blow on this spark and up it flares. Thus we are called to fan the flame of holiness through such readily available means as prayer, sacraments, living faith, loving fellowship, serving the poor, praise and worship. The more flame the more we become ablaze with the image, teachings and Spirit of Christ. Like silver and gold refined by the fire, our lives become aglow with the fire of His love (cf. Is 48:10). We become holy because we are consumed into the Holy One, becoming one with/in Him. The Church is holy because it is rooted in Jesus, who is holy. From this holiness comes vision, a vision rooted in the life of Christ and our exper-ience of the Holy Spirit who gives us this life to be our own.

We travel a sacred way in Christ, a way of awesome simplicity, honesty and freedom. Jesus is our way and the Holy Spirit is our guide. Jesus gazed upon the heart of Matthew, mired in the dirty money-politics of his time, and with the power of simplicity said to the tax collector,

"Follow me!" (cf. Lk 5:27). That is, do what I do. Imitate me. Become one with/in me. Stay close and learn of me. With and through me become the word of God spoken in a world deafened by indulgence, the noisy pursuit of money and honors, and a host of other worldly allurements that insidiously lead to enslavement. Let go of them. Be detached. Come and follow. Allow God's wisdom to be made flesh. And you will be free in heart and mind to embrace the joyous freedom that is divine life. A peace will come to rule your heavy heart and make it a dancing heart, new and bright with hope, faith and a deep love for the purity of creation. Matthew dropped his good paying government job and took up a new labor, a labor of love in the companion-ship of the Master. Matthew's apostolic friend Paul reminds us therefore to keep our eyes fixed on Jesus (cf. Heb 12:2). What did He do? Say? Show? Live? Teach? Follow Him! Let His teachings and spirit dwell richly within (cf. Col 3:16). Imitate Him. Become one with/in Him. And so we start. But soon we stumble under the weight of our own sins and those that surround us. It is the way of the cross so we get up again in order to overcome more sins. And we keep getting up. Soon the stumbles are converted from discour-agement to a deeper commitment to do and be better. And through the Great Reminder, the Holy Spirit, we remember that the way of the cross ends in victory not defeat. It is a triumphant way to overcome sin and the worldly darkness of man's inhumanity to man. So we walk with Blessed Mother Mary, Simon, Veronica and all the triumphant saints who have followed the Master on His way of the Holy Cross throughout these many centuries. A power flows from this cross that gives victory over defeat, joyfulness over sadness, assurance over doubt, light over darkness, and life over death. In this power we keep walking and follow. It is victory. Jesus is Victory!

Lord Jesus you inspire and perfect our faith as we enter ever more fully into your way and life. Each step with you is victory. And each victory warms our heart with gratitude and the joy of new life. Help us to keep walking with you, as did the Blessed Mother, apostles and saints. May we become ablaze with your holiness.

Feeding on the Living Bread

It is for us to feed on the Living Bread. Through the power of the Holy Spirit, Jesus turns ordinary bread and wine into His very body and blood. Just as He turned water into choice wine for the wedding guests at Cana. Once again the bread is multiplied and the Miracle Maker feeds His followers. The living body of Christ on earth, His people, receive the Living Body of Christ Triumphant. We become one: in, through and with Him. We are in communion. It is a celebration that is ours at every Mass. Through the transforming power of the Holy Spirit we become what we receive and celebrate what we have received by giving it to others as the living body of Christ. The Body of Christ is to be received and lived in faith. It is gift and mystery. But it is also real and true. *My body is true food. The one who feeds on me will have life because of me (Jn. 6:55-57).* It is for us to feed on this true food so that the mystical body of Christ may be manifested and made incarnate. We become one with Christ through our communion, and with His sacrificial and merciful love within us extend His presence to others. The real food received is to be further manifested through real deeds of charity in the name of Christ. The love received is to be communicated to others in deeds but also through the core of our being that quietly and humbly says, "I am one with the Lord within and I want to share the gift of this Oneness with you." Through our communion with the Lord we can become Eucharist to others. Like Christ we are broken and given away to others. We allow Christ to multiply our daily bread and transform it into meaningful feedings for others in need. One of the most poignant spiritual voices of our times, Henri Nouwen, says this to us: "You and I would dance for joy were we to know truly that we, little people, are chosen, blessed, and broken to become the bread that will multiply itself in the giving... As those who are chosen, blessed, broken and given, we are called to live our lives with a deep inner joy and peace."[15]

In feeding on Jesus we gain the power to love and not be anxious, to see and think without deception, forgive and be forgiven, trust without fully understanding, praise God and not curse the world. The power gained enables us to survive social pressures that would draw us away from God and His ways. The Living Bread enables us to receive and respond to His holy life. We rejoice in the Lord within us, are patient in the midst of trials, and stay focused on Him by praying always (cf. Rom 12:12). Our yoke is joined to Jesus, who is meek, gentle and obedient of heart (cf. Mt 11:29). We travel with Him along with all the saints,

---

15 Henri J. M. Nouwen, Life of the Beloved, Spiritual Living in a Secular World, Crossroad Publishing, N.Y., 1996, Pp. 99 and 103.

past and present. We believe in His Lordship and words, become leaven wherever we go, and allow God to draw good from all things (cf. Rom 8:28). Our lives become an extension of the celebration of the Mass in which the Crucified and Risen Christ is offered for the redemption of the world. The Living Bread received is the living bread given and multiplied in His Holy Name.

Lord Jesus upon you we feed that you may also feed others through us. May we become what we receive, and give to others what we receive in holy Eucharist. In further realizing and living this, we truly give thanks and fulfill what Eucharist means.

A Wide Call and Narrow Path

God's call to holiness is universal. His gifts to accomplish it abide and abound. But it leads to a narrow path. The call is to come to God Himself and it goes out to each of us. The gift of the call and means to satisfy it are not taken back (cf. Rom 11:29). They are always there. We can refuse to respond and use the gifts that God extends. We can fail to see with renewed minds and hear with clean hearts the purity and personal love of His call. The call is gentle yet persistent, freeing rather than enslaving, and inclusive rather than exclusive in nature. Every human creature is invited to share in the holiness of the Creator. His personal call is spoken in His teachings, and powerfully and uniquely communicated in His Eucharistic body and blood. It is echoed in the lives and witness of the saints, and seen in compassionately serving the needs of the poor. His call is deeply and mysteriously experienced in hearts that are quiet and stilled by the wonder of silence. It is exclaimed in personal mind-body-spirit healing, and gloriously announced with each bright sunrise and glowing sunset. Hearts opened to the Holy Spirit prayerfully acknowledge it.

The wonder of the expansiveness of such a persistent personal call inebriates us. God's greatness, infinite creativity and personal love overwhelm us. That is what they are meant to do! Wherever we turn, He is still there calling us to Himself. Though the means abide and are wide, the response draws us to a narrow path that affords little desire or spare time in which to wander.

Our Lord Jesus gradually but powerfully becomes our focus, the inspirer and perfecter of our faith. Our lives begin to be patterned after His and with St. Paul we begin to realize that it is Christ living in us and perfecting us. *I live no longer I, but Christ lives in me; insofar as I now live in the flesh, I live by faith in the Son of God, who has loved me and given himself up to me (Gal 2:20).* The idolatry of worldly measures of success, enmity, strife, jealousy, anger, selfishness, dissension, envy, carousing and similar works of the walk in the flesh cited by St. Paul diminish and eventually disappear as we take our walk in the Spirit of Christ (cf. Gal 5:16-21). It is a walk of love that is sharply focused on the selfless image and likeness of Christ Jesus. With grace we gradually come to think, love, and breathe Jesus. In embracing and living such a focus, we realize that this narrow path leads and opens us to an embrace of all humanity in His holy name and grace. And the wonder of it all goes on, grace upon grace (cf. Jn. 1:16). Truly with and through Jesus grace has entered our world to transform us.

We can open ourselves to the Spirit of God being poured forth into our hearts and lives (cf. Rom. 5:5) or we can say *no* to any or all of it. But the call and gifts remain. In saying *yes* to the call and gifts, however, our focus is sharpened and we see life differently than those whose wide path embraces so many disparate worldly attractions and pursuits. We are led to *invest* time in Christ-centered things and development rather than *spending* time on a multitude of worldly satisfactions that never really satisfy.

With wisdom we come to embrace a long-term view with an incomparable yield rather than succumbing to a multitude of immediate but passing gratifications. Our transformed lives carry a commission to speak and live God's immutable way to a rapidly changing world. We can show to others that things that do not change and are of God are to be *more* valued than things of mankind that never stop changing. Our challenge and commission is to give a Christ-axis and meaning to a spinning world of change. The modern technological thrust has in particular applied greater velocity to the spinning world of change and provided us with a wider variety of troublesome wobbles and misdirections. More than ever a Christ-axis of stability is needed so that whatever advances are made become part of the fabric of a better or more moral world. Otherwise humanity will only use others for selfish gain rather than for the common good and God's glory. The opportunities and ways are many. But only one leads to life everlasting. Christ has come to show us that way. Let us choose the narrow way that opens to the free and everlasting way. It is Christ who stands at the door knocking and inviting us to the narrow way that His church guides and nourishes with God-given gifts and authority. It is for us to choose the narrow and disciplined way. So few seek it. So few find it. Yet it is the way Home.

Lord Jesus your yoke is easy and your burden light as we walk with and in you to life everlasting. The way is straight, narrow and sure when we submit to your gentle touch and direction. In doing so we submit to success not failure, fellowship not isolation, and abundance not deprivation.

Only a Reflective Life is Worth Living

Only a reflective life is worth living. It alone moves us to a lasting dimension and experience instead of just a passing one. A contemplative mind and heart affords this deeper vision and experience. The velocity of the active world alone would suggest the glaring need for reflection and contemplation. What the contemporary world seems to need most is "speed bumps" to slow us lest we run over and kill too many good things along the way, including ourselves. More is not always better. Faster does not always get us there. *Festina lente* we hear echoed from the ages past of Cicero: *Make haste slowly!* Real progress and advancement do not come quickly. It takes time. Sometimes lots of it. In our daily rush of life, time itself becomes the most precious currency. Yet we remain ever poorer as we take on more and more and run faster and faster. The computer, cell phones and other devices that were to save us time and energy propel us to an even faster track and further dispersion and loss of inner energy. The crowds gather around us ever larger, faster and more verbose.

The crowds gathered around Jesus and the apostles seeking more and more, faster and faster. But Jesus told his disciples then and now to "come aside." Get some rest. Pray. Reflect on what is happening. Prayerfully think about *why* it is happening and *how* it should happen. Don't be scattered. Be collected. Walk deliberately but prayerfully. Don't get swept away to be owned by the crowds. You are to be precious leaven that will raise the crowd above its madness of fickle movement, velocity and ferocious noise.

Come aside and be quiet. Walk in the collected quiet of an inner self re-energized by God's grace. Be sensitive to getting scattered by the rush of events and people. Remember to come aside and rest in Christ. It is for us to enter the inner sanctuary of God's intimate presence that invites us to know and see that His Spirit refreshes us and gives us new life. We need rest stops along the way. Daily! Meditation and contemplation provide the inner rest needed. It clears our vision and makes it Christ-centered. It empowers us to be balanced and free to serve the needs of our times. In fact it *better* equips us to serve the needs of our times because we are free of the consuming self and better able to reach out to those in need.

Contemplative, reflective living equips us to walk calmly, focused, and at times even miraculously. St Peter has much to teach us about keeping our gaze upon Jesus. *"Lord, if it is you, command me to come to you on the water," Peter asks (Mt 14:28).* And Our Lord let Him walk on water to get to Him. But the stormy seas around Peter distracted his eyes of faith, and the lack of focus soon plunged Peter into the sea. Like Peter the storms of the world around us easily distract our eyes and we loose our focus on the One whose strength and love enable us to walk calmly on the water instead of drowning in it. Christ alone can give us the calmness within that empowers us to walk on the waters of daily life without sinking in the complexities and turbulence around us.

Lord Jesus with Peter may we learn to keep the eyes of our hearts and minds focused on you at all times. Grant us the grace to do this. In faith we come to you. In trust we are embraced by you.

Epilogue

Rooted in Christ, our story is in time yet is timeless. The saga continues, with or without words. While it is true that we cannot adequately speak about God, it is equally true that we cannot be silent about Him. The mystery we live is meant more to be experienced than explained. Yet it deserves to be articulated and proclaimed so that we may better know, access and experience the gift of new life in the Spirit of Christ. It is in sharing and further living this that we become more in His Holy Name. While it is true that Christ lives within and amongst us, there is more to come. The best is yet to be. The end is just the beginning as we live and share this life in the Spirit of Christ.

You are strangers and aliens no longer. No you are fellow citizens of the saints and members of the household of God. You form a building, which rises on the foundation of the apostles and prophets, with Christ Jesus himself as the capstone. Through him the whole structure is fitted together and takes shape as a holy temple in the Lord; in him you are being built into this temple, to become a dwelling place for God in the Spirit.

—Ephesians 2:19-22

Resource and Reference

- An Anatomy and Discussion of Prayer
- Annotated List of Related Readings

An Anatomy and Discussion of Prayer

The Power and Many Faces of Prayer

Prayer is a turning to God: a turning to the Source of our being and eternal life. It is our lifeline to God and human way to personally participate in divine life. There are many ways in which we do this.

We pray corporately and individually, publicly and privately, in song and silence, with friends and alone, in church community and lonely places, with minds and hearts, in times of celebration and crisis. We pray with our whole lives and total being in the never ending transition of life to prayer and prayer to life until, by God's grace and our cooperation, they become one in time or eternity.

There are many methods and faces of prayer. In hand with the Blessed Mother we pray the rosary and find it to be a powerful way to stay close to the life of Jesus through Mary. There are favorite novenas to keep us focused on our friends, the saints, and through their intercession gain strength and assistance in times of special need. The liturgy joins us to the prayer and sacrifice of Jesus as we share in the sacramental offering of Himself for and to us in the Holy Mass. We pray with words and without words, with thoughts and without thoughts, in a meditative and contemplative way.

Distinguishing Main Lines of Prayer

Two distinguishing main lines of prayer are **_kataphatic_** and **_apophatic_**: with words and thoughts, and without words and concepts. They respectively embrace discursive and unknowing, concentrative and receptive, active and resting, as well as filling and emptying in nature and approach. The kataphatic and apophatic approaches are fundamentally different yet share a common Spirit as their source and serve to complement and nourish one another. They occupy different places in our lives at different times.

The Christ-centered life explored in this book focuses more on the receptive-resting (*apophatic*) rather than the concentrative-active (*kataphatic*) prayer approach. It seeks to develop more of a letting go (detached) view of prayer and daily life than the controlling and concentrative emphasis and direction. It postulates a *being* rather than *doing* approach and perception of prayer and life. It also recognizes that a more simple and receptive approach is more difficult to develop and sustain, especially in the midst of such a challenging culture and times. The dependence is more upon God rather than ourselves as the means of moving forward. It is more a matter of: waiting upon God to act and reveal Himself than actively acquiring and eliciting His presence and will; allowing God the time, way and place in which to act and direct rather than taking well thought out preemptive action that then seeks God's affirmation; and finally it embraces the fundamental realization that it really is God's work in prayer and life that matters most and is most worthy of preeminence.

Our rich Christian and Catholic tradition honors and upholds both the kataphatic and apophatic views of prayer and the associated life posture that they emphasize and make incarnate.

Simple and Infused Contemplative Prayer: Dimensions and Methods

The many dimensions of kataphatic prayer share the common thread of active thought and concentration that serve to gain and sustain the knowledge and experience of God's presence. The rosary, novenas, vocal and meditative prayers, liturgy, imaging prayer are some examples. Activity of the mind and thought, voice and body are integral to this form. But in contemplation, and the apophatic tradition from which it prescinds, there is a radical shift to inner stillness and reception of God's gift of His presence. In faith and love, waiting and calm, the approach that we call Centering Prayer begins with consenting to God's gratuitous presence as He chooses to bestow Himself. It is a *surrender to* rather than an acquiring or conquering of God's presence. Simple contemplation and the entry method of Centering Prayer recognizes that while our intention (*desire*) is required, it nevertheless is God's work not ours that brings forth the transcending experience of

God's presence. God controls the movement. We simply *let it* happen by totally surrendering ourselves to rest in God's will and presence. Our place in Centering Prayer is to position ourselves to receive God's gift of His transcending and transforming presence. We choose to close the door to our ego and self-centeredness in order to become centered on and in God alone. Our gaze and focus are on God in waiting and loving stillness. We gladly acknowledge that God's grace makes it happen. Only the transcendent yet immanent one who dwells deeply within can give us the experience that transcends our limited and finite self. Only God can unite us with Himself and make us one with and in Him. The gift is His to bestow and ours to receive.

In the emptying and abandonment of the false self (ego) comes the true self and exaltation of God's oneness. In faith and love we consent to receiving and coming into communion with God who is infinite love. How and when Infused Contemplation – the Gift and unmanipulated experience of God Himself – actually happens is beyond us. But the infused experience provides the indelible affirmation and confirmation of the power and peace of the Gift received and known. And we know experientially that it transcends a self-induced or intellectual exercise and experience. Words and thoughts fail to grasp and describe the gift realized in Infused Contemplation. It is a gratuitous gift from God, utterly controlled by Him. By faith's consent we are led into the reality of Infinite Love. And the experience of this Love serves to transform us, eventually transforming our attitude, perceptions, thoughts, and actions in daily life.

Centering Prayer

Centering Prayer begins with God's presence within us. We simply consent to the reality of this presence in faith and love. In stillness we surrender our thoughts, words and being to the Risen Christ who makes His home within us through our consent, and embraces us as He wills with His transcen-dent loving presence. It is a death-to-life experience: a movement from the finite to the infinite, and even more deeply from our nothingness to God's all. And it is Christ-centered, led and controlled. St. Paul refers to Christ as the leader and perfecter of our faith (Heb 12:2). The way of Christ described by St. Paul in his letter to the Philippians holds eloquent meaning and application to the approach and practice of Centering Prayer:

> *Let this mind be in you that was in Christ Jesus, who though he was in the form of God did not regard equality with God as something to be exploited, but emptied himself taking the form of a slave, being born in human*

> *likeness. And being found in human likeness, he humbled himself and became obedient to the point of death — even death on a cross. Therefore God also highly exalted him. (Phil. 2:5-9)*

The Centering provides the entry method into contemplation that leads to the Infused Contemplation in which God raises us to an experience of His divine place and life that transcends words, our understanding, and capability.

> *For my thoughts are not your thoughts, nor are your ways my ways says the Lord. For as the heavens are higher than the earth, so are my ways higher than your ways and my thoughts than your thoughts. (Is 55:8)*

In the acceptance of this realization, Centering Prayer strives to put aside our own thoughts and ways in order to rest and be in the way and presence of the Risen Christ dwelling within and beyond us.

The Centering method of prayer is the most simple of all and leads to the purest practice and experience of prayer. But it certainly is not the easiest. It requires the deepest part of us (*our heart*), and abiding commitment (*our discipline*). It is a movement of grace that takes time and it is not cheap. Yet the yield is priceless and changes our life, if we consent to it.

In Lectio Divina (*divine reading*), the kataphatic approach is uniquely combined with the apophatic. The movement is from reading (*lectio*) to meditation (*meditatio*) to prayer (*oratio*) to contemplation (*contemplatio*). The Lectio method into contemplation deserves separate and further discussion but we will leave that for other readings and writings. In contrast, the Centering Prayer approach is exclusively apophatic in nature and method. Nevertheless it shares the same goal of contemplative resting in the Lord, though it follows a more direct way of getting there. Lectio and Centering serve to nourish, strengthen and deepen one's experience of the Living God and thus are complementary disciplines and gifts. Most importantly they lead us into a deep resting in God that is reserved for those who believe: *For we who have believed enter into that rest, just as God has said (Heb 4:3)*. Resting in God is the very essence of Contemplative Prayer. It is the Gift that Centering Prayer opens and prepares us to receive.

The roots of Centering Prayer reach deeply into our Christian contemplative heritage as practiced and taught by such great spiritual masters as the saints Teresa of Avila and John of the Cross. Through the work of modern masters of prayer, Centering was developed in an effort to present the rich teachings of the earlier masters into more current form and accessibility. They include the prolific writings and teachings of Cistercian Fathers Thomas Keating and Basil Pennington, and Thomas Merton who gave the name "centering" to this method of prayer. "The focus of Centering Prayer is the deepening of our relationship with the living Christ," states Father Thomas Keating in his instructional pamphlet on the Method of Centering Prayer, the Prayer of Consent.[16]

---

[16] A copy of the instructional pamphlet by Father Thomas Keating on The Method of Centering Prayer, The Prayer of Consent is available through Contemplative Outreach, Ltd. 10 Park Place P.O. Box 737, Butler, N.J. 07405 Tel. 973-838-3384, Fax: 973-492-5795, Email: office@coutreach.org

Annotated Reference List of Related Readings

The related readings in this section are rich soil in which to plant one's study and practice of a prayerful Christ-centered life. It is a privilege to recommend them to you.

INWARD STILLNESS
By Fr. George Maloney, S.J.
— Dimension Books, Denville, N.J.

A masterful, clear, scholarly and scriptural presentation of the mysterious art of communicating with God that stimulates and guides the reader to enter deeply into the inner world of immanence "where God communicates in a language of love that has to be experienced beyond words, concepts, images or even emotional feelings."

TOWARD GOD
By Fr. Michael Casey, OCSO
— Liguori/Triumph, Liguori, MO.

Recaptures an ancient approach to contemplative prayer that makes it a way of life, a communion with God that is meant to be lived. It includes the nature of contemplative prayer and conditions necessary for its authenticity.

* THE HERMIT * THE PROPHET * THE MYSTIC
By David Tarkington
— Alba House/St Paul's, New York

A trilogy on the deepening of one's prayer life that draws upon the writings and experiences of St. John of the Cross and St. Theresa of Avila on portraying the movement of spiritual life from charismatic prayer to mystical prayer.

THE COLLECTED WORKS OF ST. JOHN OF THE CROSS
Translated by Fathers Kavanaugh and Rodriquez, OCD
— ICS Publications, Washington, D. C.

Presents a deeper understanding and appreciation of the teachings of the Mystical Doctor, St. John of the Cross, whose intention was to teach souls the dynamics of growth in union with God.

CLOUD OF UNKNOWING AND THE BOOK OF PRIVY COUNSEING
Edited with an introduction by Fr. William Johnson
— Doubleday Image, N. Y.

A modern edition of the 14th Century spiritual classic, offering a practical guide on the path of contemplation.

CONTEMPLATIVE PRAYER
By Fr. Thomas Merton, O.C.S.O.
— Doubleday Image, New York

A clear, expansive and instructive exploration of contemplative prayer by a well revered modern Master and prolific writer.

NEW SEEDS OF CONTEMPLATION
By Fr. Thomas Merton, O.C.S.O.
— New Directions, New York

Awakens dormant inner depths of the spirit to nurture a deeply contemplative and mystical dimension in our spiritual lives.

THOUGHTS IN SOLITUDE
By Fr. Thomas Merton, O.C.S.O.
— Farrar, Straus and Company, New York

Stimulating reflections stemming from Merton's previous writing of Seeds of Contemplation and his life and love of silence and solitude.

OPEN MIND OPEN HEART
By Fr. Thomas Kealing, O.C.S.O.
— Amity House, Warwick, N.Y.

An overview of Christian contemplative prayer and detailed guidance in the method of Centering Prayer.

INVITATION TO LOVE
By Fr. Thomas Keating, O.C.S.O.
— Continuum, New York

A thorough presentation of the Spiritual Journey that begins with the study and practice of Centering Prayer.

INTIMACY WITH GOD
By Fr. Thomas Keating, O.C.S.O.
— Continuum, New York

A deeper understanding of the Spiritual Journey and transformation through contemplation.

CALL TO THE CENTER
By Fr. Basil Pennington, O.C.S.O.
— New City Press, New York

A refreshing collection of short meditations on the Gospel of Matthew, and an invitation to enter the prayer of the heart—Centering Prayer.

CENTERED LIVING
By Fr. Basil Pennington, O.C.S.O.
— Liguori/Triumph, Liguori, MO

Testimonies of practioners, updated guidelines, theological reflections and helpful hints about Centering Prayer.

A TASTE FOR SILENCE
By Fr. Carl Aruzo
— Continuum, New York

An illuminating guide of the fundamentals of Centering Prayer and advancement toward a deeper spirituality.

HE LEADETH ME
By Fr. Walter Ciszek, S.J.
— Ignatius Press, San Francisco

A powerful and instructive personal account of a spiritual odyssey that comes to rest in unflagging faith and total reliance on God's will that brings forth the comfort of spiritual contemplation, inner serenity and victory over all things – even the evil that surrounded Father Ciszek in a Soviet prison.

ABANDONMENT TO DIVINE PROVIDENCE
By Fr. Jean Pierre de Caussade
— Doubleday Image Book

A spiritual classic that illuminates the sacredness of each moment and consequential need of abandonment to God's will in all things.

HOUSING HEAVEN'S FIRE, THE CHALLENGE OF HOLINESS
By Fr. John Haughey, S.J.
— Loyola Press, Chicago

An insightful scriptural pilgrimage and exploration of what it means to be holy. The focus is on Jesus as the best example of holiness embodied, and an invitation to accept the challenge of holiness that Jesus affords in our every day life.

FOLLOWING JESUS
By N. T. Wright
— William Eerdmans Publishing Co., Grand Rapids, MI.

Biblical reflections on discipleship and what it means to follow Jesus today. It challenges us to look to the real Jesus, the pioneer and perfecter of our faith who endured the cross and hostility.

GUIDE TO LIVING IN THE TRUTH
By Fr. Michael Casey, O.C.S.O.
— Liguori/Triumph, Liguori, MO.

Addresses the human condition and shows how humility embodies a happiness and power of freedom that enables us to effectively cope with external difficulties and sorrows, and provides a sure path to happiness in Christ.

TURNED TO THE LORD
By Thaddeus Horgan
— Franciscan Federation, Pittsburgh, PA.

A portrait of St. Francis of Assisi whose only model was the Incarnate Christ and guide was the book of the gospels. Francis took on the poverty and humility of Jesus and gave to us a living example of Our Lord Christ to follow.

JESUS OF NAZARETH
By Pope Benedict XVI
— Doubleday

A scholarly, insightful, scriptural look at Jesus emanating from many years of study, reflection and experience in serving and preaching Jesus the Christ, in whom we find our identity and communion with God the Father.

Living in a World of Contingency and Upheaval

We are walking in unprecedented times struggling with a worldwide virus that has claimed millions of lives and threatens more. It claimed the jobs of some 30 million USA workers, that placed us in an economic recession equal to the Great Depression of 1933, shut down our churches, closed our schools and told us to shelter in place. By 2021 it accounted for 500,000 deaths in the United States.

With all our brilliant technological expertise we struggle how to deal with it, or how long it will last. It is dark inside! Hope, Humility, Trust, Collaboration, Goodness, Kindness... now shed their light on our daily lives, as neighbors help neighbors and share what they have. If ever we needed to turn to God, it is now.

As a consequence, with the COVID-19 struggle, many neighbors and organizations are partnering with one another. Who would have thought that creating physical distance would be an authentic way to care for our neighbors?

The Pandemic has opened the awareness of many. The Corona Virus has been difficult, painful, and deadly as thousands died of infectious COVID-19 disease. In order to abide by the demands of distancing, many of the churches were closed as have our schools. Government restrictions at many levels inflicted their restrictions in a multifaceted effort to contain the spread of COVID-19 virus in the midst of millions exposed to what could be and was deadly in many cases. The elderly was quarantined as they were the most exposed to the virus strains and capable of exposing others accordingly.

The world was being torn apart by thousands deaths and disorders of every kind. Suddenly millions were out of work. Many, however, preserved their jobs by being allowed to work at home. Many were able to adopt a more reflective mode while off the commuter travel road. Also in a positive sense, it served to bring forth a newness of fathering for prayer, and other religious groups to gather in efficacious ways via technological means.

ZOOM arrangements connected pray-ers for common prayers, instruction, and dialogue to address theological issues, religious matters, scriptural wisdom and sharing. It also introduced or reminded many to realize the contingency and instability of the world we are living in. what seemed so orderly and economically strong can and does pass out of being in just a few days as social distancing restrictive quarantines, sheltering in place upset our daily lives. The Good News is that as followers of Christ, our strength and trust is found and placed in God and his Church which is the Rock that is not shattered as so many lives have been in crisis. The mixture of disruptive job losses, school and business closures, and unending social demonstrations taking place so rapidly all over the globe has cast a darkness and divisiveness over us. Nevertheless, a bright light has been shining in the midst of the 2020 Pandemic: The social heroic services given to so many people in critical need of health care professionals, community, volunteers, military personnel, churches and many others who strive to Help and Love one another in what has become a solidarity of goodness. St. Thomas Aquinas has said that Goodness is diffusive of itself. That is to say: Goodness has to give itself away. The more it gives of itself the bigger it gets. As professionals give of themselves, the more they want to give in helping the COVID-19 patients. They were all striving to do God's work by offering their healing services. Looking at the unselfish labors that reached out to those in need brought forth much applause, media attention, and the poser of helping those in need. Many service organizations helped to assist the health care workers. All involved were and are worthy of the recognition of being such luminary and exemplary witnesses of God.

The Church seen as the Rock, is not shattered as so many lives have been in these crisis around the world. The mixture of disruptive job losses, school and business closures, with unending social demonstrations taking place so rapid all over the globe, has caused a darkness and divisiveness over us. Nevertheless, a bright light has been shining in the midst of the 2020 Pandemic. The heroic services given to people in critical need by healthcare professionals, community volunteers, military personnel, churches and many others who strive to Help and Love one another in what has become a solidarity of goodness. This goodness, spread across the globe, gave us immense light in the midst of the darkness of pain. The more the health professionals gave of themselves, the more they wanted to give in helping the

COVID-19 patients in their suffering as the nurses and doctors saw so many of the patients die. The healthcare personnel were striving to do God's work by fully offering their services over many long days and nights, looking at the unselfish laborer who reached out to those in need. Many service agencies helped to assist the healthcare workers. All involved were worthy of the recognition for being such luminary and exemplary witnesses.

Living in a New World

*T**he world we know is a contingent one. It presents a magnitude of profound natural changes that surround us. All that we see around us in a natural and human manner will change and ultimately pass away. It can change dramatically and quickly. Currently we are in a particular unprecendented time in 2021 that has been darkened by the COVID-19 pandemic. The deadly COVID-19 infection spread quickly across the globe claiming thousands of deaths daily. In a few months, the world posted millions of COVID deaths. All were and are in danger across the world as medical doctors and scientists struggled with the multitudes seeking proper care, new prevention protocols and other needs to effectively deal with the explosion of those infected by the deadly power of the virus.*

The medical experts and scientists did not have a vaccine to stop the strange COVID-19. What was known immediately was that the DEADLY virus spread quickly and was best for all to avoid large culture events. Social distancing helped to contain the spread. Government restrictions were imposed to further reduce contagion. Soon, restaurants, business sporting events, schools and, yes churches were closed. Further protocols were articulated by top scientists, especially Dr. Anthony Fauci of the National Institutes of Health who particularly pushed that masks be used in public to avoid the spread of the virus. Travels became limited between states. As businesses were closing some 30 million jobs were lost and an economic recession equal to the Great Depression of 1933 was upon us.

We all learned about contingency: economic, social, closing schools and other interruptions along with other changes that altered our daily life. We also learned that closing churches brought forth some misguided solutions.

The failure of the general public to listen to the proven experts can be deadly, and yield bug numbers. Looking back in world history, the other major pandemic that occurred in 1918 has already been exceeded by the number of COVID deaths in the United States. What all this says is that we need to pay attention to what Jesus Christ taught us in living our daily lives and what our churches can do to further help one another, and make this country and world we live in much better place for all of us.

I want to share with you a few lines from the original texts (pages 7, 8, 9): Living in the Truth. The reality we kjow deeply and live truthfully is the reality of Christ within us……Christ has irrevocably joined humanity and divinity, living within yet transcending our humanity. Though humanity remains humanity and God remains God, we are invited through grace to participate more fully in the divine life.

From Pope Francis, General Audience, 30 September (CNEWA's World):

"A small virus continues to cause deep wounds and expose our physical, social and spiritual vulnerabilities …....Inspired by the Holy Spirit, we can work together for the Kingdom of God that Christ inaugurated in this world by coming among us. It is a kingdom of light in the midst of darkness, of justice in the midst of so many outrages, of joy in the midst of so much pain, if healing and salvation in the midst of sickness and death of tenderness in the midst of hatred. May God grant us to 'viralize love and globalize hope in the light of faith."

Social distancing helped to limit exposure to the virus, and washing hands and staying away from large crowds helped to curtain the spread. Governmental restrictions were imposed to further reduce contagion. Soon, restaurants, businesses, large cultural events, schools and yes, churches were closed. The elderly was quarantined as they were the most exposed to the virus strain and capable of exposing others. We were and are learning that there are many changes to be made in our daily lifestyles, needs and precautions. ***We are indeed living in a new world.***

The Spirit of Christ

The Spirit of Christ is the center of our lives. But we are looking upon the current world that is broken, frightened with thousands of COVID-19 deaths each day in the United States, and a fractured world that is broken in many ways. The Scriptures tell us, "No one knows what pertains to God except the Spirit of God" (1Cor. 2:11 – 13); Following Pentecost, it was Peter who stood up with the Eleven Apostles and proclaimed what the Profit Joel had said "it will come to pass in the last days that I will pour out a portion of my spirit all the flesh and will work wonders in the heaven above and signs on earth below" (Acts 2:14 – 19). If there ever were a need of prayer for our nation and world, it is PRAYER NOW. That prayer can take the form of active prayer helping the poor, feeding families who do not have food or water, those without shelter, those who are without employment …..... those who are in need! They are called neighbors whether they live close by in the same country or village or village across the country. The questions was: WHAT WOULD JESUS DO? How can we who are in good health help those who are struggling with COVID-19? Let us keep our minds, heart and prayers open and alive.

God's Grace and Love

We know that all of Scripture originates in God. We also know that all things work together for good for those who love God and are called according to his purpose (Romans 8:28). In reflecting on the Old Testament, we can see the word of law being spoken by God to His People, predominantly calling to them to be obedient to Him. In the New Testament, Jesus Christ is the Son of God and the New Man. Indeed, in word, He is the Word of God. As the Gospel of John says, the law was given through Moses in the Old Testament, but Grace and Truth, came through Jesus Christ. From His fullness we have all received grace upon grace (John 1:16 – 18). How blessed we are in the New Testament to know and hopefully live the word that God bestows on us. While the word of God was given to us in the Old Testament through Moses and the kings, prophets and psalms, God chose to send His Own Son to BE the Word. The Old Testament was and is Holy, but in the New Testament the Word is perfected in the Person of Jesus Christ and the Saints. A beautiful and totally unique holiness came into our world when the Person of Jesus Christ took on our natural world to show and tell us what is right and lasting life. If we chose to share and participate in life eternal, it begins NOW. And learn to better live in accordance with God's will and sustained faith. Our call is to believe, adore, and have hope and love. And pray for those who do not believe, adore and have hope and love. Our blessed Mother Mary has much to teach us in that regard in our journey to being more rooted in the Sacred Heart of Jesus through the Immaculate Heart of Mary.

(Prayer) ....Lord Jesus and Holy Mary we yearn and beg for your grace to better know and live a life of holiness that reflects your love and reach every more for the eternal stretch that fills our hearts and helps us to better see and count on the faith in the life that awaits us above.

Solidarity of Goodness Grows in our Land

The church is a Rock that has not shattered as so many lives have in the 2020/21 Pandemic crisis. On the contrast, it has come forth to provide moral and spiritual and prayer strength for those lives that were disrupted by the pandemic. Attending to the thousands of COVID-19 cases during the pandemic in the many hospitals across the land and world were the heroic services of the nurses, doctors and health care professionals, and yes scientists who reached out to provide health care guidance, and hope needed to get their patients back on their feet and returned to their loved ones at home. The applause offered by the whole world was authentic and filled by joy and love. These heroes deserved the recognition many times over. They provided the light of Goodness to the thousands who were suffering so deeply in the darkness. And joining the care were the military, police, ministers, rabbis, priests, and churches who reached out to the COVID-19 patients and saving work of the heroes. There was and is a power of Goodness generated by solidarity of Goodness that permeated and brightened the scene in the hospitals. St. Thomas Aquinas has said that Goodness is diffusive of itself. That is to say, Goodness has to give itself away. There is such a goodness and joy within the heroes that they have to give it away. And in doing so, it gets Bigger! The heroes were striving to do God's work by offering their services. Seeing their unselfishness, other service organizations stepped forward to help health care workers, providing luminary and exemplary witness to Christ Jesus.

A Christ Centered Way Appears

Pope Francis delivered his 2020 report Urbi et Orbi (City and World) in a unique setting: He chose to deliver his message at St. Peter Square to an empty silent square on a rainy day standing at the foot of the gigantic Crucified Cross of Christ, praying to Christ Jesus. It was an eloquent portrayal of the seriousness of the Pandemic that was raging in so many lands in which Christ Jesus was being crucified around to the world to the One who was able to accept and transform suffering: Jesus Christ. It is our Catholic belief that God the Father sent his only begotten Son to lead us to the heavenly kingdom through the power of the Holy Spirit. Our Pope Francis published his first book entitled In Him Alone is Our Hope. The book opens the Way of Christ Jesus that leads to the heavenly kingdom as it was seen and experienced by St. Ignatius Loyola. It presents the Lord Jesus' way of life with his Law of Love that embraces Poverty, Humility and Service, if we choose the Kingdom of Heaven rather than the kingdom of the world with its values of Wealth, Vanity and Pride. In doing so we must make a discernment that qualitatively transcends all the knowledge and know how that positive sciences can offer because it draws its power from the very originality of the Gospel (In Him Alone is Our Hope, Page 34). That is to say it draws its graced power from the Love of Christ Jesus who is the Word of God (Jn1) that is spoken and lived for us. In knowing and living the Gospel – God's Truth – we receive the grace and faith that it embraces, and are obliged to pass it on. Pope Francis tells us, liberating potential of our faith does not stem from ideologies but precisely its contact with what is holy and is a manifestation of the sacred (ibid, p.35).

Jesus is the Word of God

In coming into our humanity, Our Lord Jesus invites us to embrace his heart, knowledge, wisdom, strength, humility and merciful will. He is the Word of God, and tells us that his words are Spirit and Life. (Jn 6:63) They are born of the Spirit and give Life. St. Theresa of Calcutta titled a classic book Jesus the Word or be Spoken. (Annotated Reference in Text) .... He is the word to be spoken, lived and followed as we strive to be like Christ and all the Saints. It is structured similar to the Imitation of Christ by Thomas A. Kempis and should be read with the same confidence of a classic spiritual book. In her introduction, St. Theresa wrote, do not be afraid. There must be the cross, there must be suffering – a clear sign that Jesus has drawn you close to his heart so that he can share his suffering with you. (See the Annotated Bibliography of Related Book, found in the back of Spirit of Christ). It is true that we are called to fulfill God's Will. Scripture tells us in His Will our peace found. In doing His Will each of us becomes the Truth that it beholds. In doing so our humanity is able to receive the grace – given power of His divinity as the Lord wills it. Each day is a gift. The suffering aspects that may come with it are hard and difficult to understand. Yet it was wisely stated by Paul Pascal, Jesus did not come to explain suffering. Rather He came to fill it with His Presence! These difficult Pandemic days will all the hospitalized COVID-19 patients are hard to endure. In time we begin to know that sufferings are a living sign of the cross and leads us to Kingdom Life. May we come to better see it in that light.

His Words of Eternal Life

Our Lord's words are Spirit and Life. They come from the Holy Spirit and give Life: Only God can say that. Only God can do that. All things come to be through him. All else that we see, hear and touch is contingent and will pass away. God's wisdom and power transcends us and is Eternal. The Son of God Jesus Christ is the Word of God made flesh, full of Grace and Truth. From his fullness we have received and are able to become children of God.

The Story of our Catholic Church founded by Jesus Christ gives us a magnificent and holy account in the first and other chapters of the Gospel of St. John of what and who we are called to be in our Christian and Catholic Faith. In Chapter 5, St. John speaks about the work of the Son of God (John 5:19 – 30). **"Amen, amen, Jesus answered and said to them, "a son cannot do anything on my own. And my judgement is just because I do not seek my own will but the will of the one who sent me."**

In Chapter 6 f John's Gospel, many spectacular stories of miracles performed by Jesus are shared. **In John 6:1 – 15,**

Jesus multiplied five loaves of bread that fed 5,000 followers and collected a great surplus after all had been fed. And in (16 – 21) mention was made of Jesus walking on water. In John (22 – 20) when asked about to bread from heaven that ancestors were fed in the desert by Moses, Jesus told them it was the Father who gives true bread from heaven. The bread of God is what comes down from heaven and gives life to the world. They said to Jesus, give us this bread always! Jesus said to them "I am the bread of life; whoever comes to me will never hunger and believes in me will never thirst." And further (36 – 40) Jesus said, "I told you that although you have seen me you do not believe. Everything that the Father gives me will come to me and I will not reject anyone that comes to me because I came down from heaven not to do my own will but the will of the one who sent me ... (40) Everyone who sees the Son and believes in him may have eternal life, and I shall raise him on the last day." The Jews murmured about him and said, "Is this not Jesus, the son of Joseph? Do we not know his father and mother?"

How can he say "I came down from heaven?" (John 6:43 – 44). Jesus said "Stop murmuring, no one can come to me unless the Father who sent me draws him, and I will raise him on the Last day (45 – 52). It is written in the prophets; they shall be taught by God." Everyone who listens to my Father and learns from him comes to me. Amen, amen, I say to you who ever believes has eternal life. I am the bread of life. Your ancestors ate the manna in the desert, but they died. This is the bread that comes down from heaven; whoever eats this bread will live forever and the bread that I will give is my flesh for life of the World. How can this man give us his flesh to eat?".

(53 – 59) Jesus said to them, Amen, amen, I say to you, unless you eat the flesh of the Son of Man and drink his blood; you do not have life within you. Whoever eats my flesh and drinks my blood has eternal life and I will raise him on the last day. For my flesh is real food, and my blood is true drink. Whoever eats my flesh remains in me and in him. Just as the Father sent me and I have life because of the Father, so also the one who feeds on me will have life because of me. This is the bread that came down from heaven. Unlike your ancestors who ate and still died, whoever eats this bread will live forever. These things he said while teaching in the synagogue in Capernaum.

(60) Then many of the disciples who were listening said, "this saying is hard. Who can accept it". Jesus knew his disciples were murmuring and said to them, "Does this shock you? What if you were to see the Son of Man ascending to where he was before? It is the Spirit that gives life, but there are some of you who do not believe. For this reason, I have told you that no one can come to me unless it is granted to him by my Father."

As a result of this many of his disciples returned to their way of life and no longer accompanied him… Jesus said to the Twelve, "Do you want to leave?" Peter answered him, "Master to whom shall we go? We have come to believe and are convinced that you are the Holy One of God." Jesus answered them; did I not choose you twelve? Yet is not one of you a devil? It was Judas who would betray him.

Finding Heaven in Christ and Discovering Him in Each Other

Pope Benedict XVI says that Christ summons us to find heaven in him, to discover him in others and this to be heaven to each other. He calls us to let heaven shine into this world. Jesus stretched out his hand to us in the mystery of the sacraments, so that the light of heaven may shine forth in this world and the doors may be opened. The Church is to proclaim truth to the world, to affirm that God is, that he knows us, and that God as Jesus Christ has revealed him and given us the path of life. From Behold: The Pierced One: An Approach to a Spiritual Christology, Graham Harrison, Tr. Ignatius Press, San Francisco, CA.

www.ingramcontent.com/pod-product-compliance
Lightning Source LLC
LaVergne TN
LVHW011937070526
838202LV00054B/4701